Dreamer of Dreams

RAY DACOLIAS

Dreamer of Dreams

ISBN 978-1-942721-01-7

Contents

Unification

"I fall; always falling, my body rides an infinite down-stream of continuous motion. I float, I sail, I glide, I sift through this mad asylum, this burning night-mare that engulfs me; I have been plunged mercilessly into a monstrous black and rusted tomb, a grotesque labyrinth, this yawning vacuum of hell, where the ageless epochs of space and time seem fathomless and immortal. O, to place my feet upon the sweet solace of the soft, delicious land, to exult in the moist, green grass, to inhale the luminous cry of the exhilarating sun, to inhale the soft and rich fragrance of the land, to feel it, to love it, to know it, to understand and adore it; this is to be alive again.

"It is as if I am in a split in the realm of time, placed in an interregnum of unlimited duration, trapped in the giant womb of this hollow shell, a forgotten speck in this awful oblivion.

"I feel nothing; there is no warmth or cold, wetness or dryness, nor ecstasy or pain to my body; no growth, no dam-age, no renewal; I feel no hunger or thirst, and smell nothing; I feel no movement; I feel no substances; I feel no currents of air or beams of light. I can see nothing, taste nothing, hear nothing; only darkness descends, only stagnation, only emptiness; no color do I behold, no sensation do I experience, no melody do I enjoy.

"I ride a shapeless, matterless beam of echoless madness.

"My soul cries for the bald juice of sensation, to wallow in its breadth and width and height, to suckle at its nourishing breast, to drink its frosty and creamy sweetness, to see the gorgeous complexion of the world adorned in golden hues and velvet fabric and violet-soaked glimmerings.

"I do not sleep.

"How long have I suffered? How do I count the days or weeks, months or years? Does the concept of time exist here? My body does not age. I feel no weariness, no illness, no weakness; all bodily functions relating to expelling waste have abated; oblivion, I have stepped inside your wretched soul.

"I remember, with vivid realization, how I came upon this accursed abyss; there, in my mind, I come upon the black hole, remembering every surrounding detail in its proper place, where every tree, bush, and shrub lie, and their color and size and fragrance. I hear the gently blowing wind, feel the warm sunshine on my bare skin, and see the clear, cerulean sky.

"I am out deep in the forest, staring into this seemingly benevolent void, which beseeches me to inspect it further. What a fool I was! I seem to lose sense of reality as I am drawn into another kind of dimension and force; and before I can choose my fate, I am violently ripped into its insidious mouth to begin the descent to this present sentence of solitary doom.

"Alas, I do not know why I have been so condemned or who my executioner is.

"Falling, falling, like the world turns: and its mighty wind that blows, and its majestic closing of night and beginning of day; I fall. This falling is part of the universe, a part of Mankind, a part of me—inseparable, constant, alive.

"O, such blessed thoughts I often construct in my benighted mind—that I avoid the grasping hand of fate and I continue homeward. And always I awaken to find the betrayals of a dream. But I know this is false, to dream; and yes, there are no tears. There is no crying here.

"Though this pestilence breathes its wicked fire through me and stabs and mutilates my flesh, it has not laid its rotting nostrils upon my mind.

"Ah, my mind; it soars, it engulfs, it spreads its golden and gleaming wings and grows, leaping past mortal thoughts, smashing human barriers, illuminating woes and enigmas and confusion; my mind, fed by the magnificent intellect of this arcane captor, lives, perceiving the way the world has been, should be, and must be, while my cold flesh dies.

"The eons pass.

"How long has it been? I ask the question and an answer, now, develops from deep within, an answer I deplore and yet cannot forget.

"One thousand years...alone...without the simple presence of human beings to comfort me, to remind me of who I still am, who I must still remain.

"What have I become? I know what I have become.

"The Earth should exist without me.

"My essence is distant and obscure, massive and smelling of grand visions, all incompatible for human beings."

* * * * *

"Something has transpired: a subtle change in the void that cradles me; and I feel it, just like the placid lake feels the entrance of the falling leaf, I feel a ripple flutter about me. Can it be? Is it possible? What am I to do? It has been so long, and I am so tired, so full of myself, so far removed from humanity that I breed contempt for those who have abandoned me.

"I panic. To be alive again, to be free, to simply exist apart from myself seems an illusion, as if it never existed. Is it even possible that I can leave my Mother, my Nurturer, my Lover and Tormentor? She who has married me to knowledge and powers not beheld by mortal man? But what good is a star that does not shine nor give warmth?

"It is over."

Rymalone Weston Augustine was expelled from the mouth of the circular chasm and gently laid to rest in a thick growth of brown bush and thick, verdant grass. He lay on his back in a profound state of uncertainty and agitation for a time that was indiscernible to him, eyes open, breath hard, his hands dug deep into the soft gush of the vibrant forest soil.

His body greedily drank in this wondrous appetite that heightened his fleshly experience, this virgin emotion that spilled into his soul, like a new organ imparting another exquisite sense, carrying his mind into a far better orbit of emotional delights than he could ever conceive.

His body trembled now, his hands moving wildly in the moist earth, his chest and stomach shivering, his countenance dancing in ecstasy; and then he tore off his clothes and shoes and socks and dug his warm toes deep into the thick dirt, his body rolling about, tossing and turning passionately. His face then fell into the pulsing mush and he smelled its provocative charms.

This sumptuous frolic lasted for an hour, at which time he clothed himself and stood upon his bare feet and approached the gorgeous trees and tender sprouts, inhaling their dynamic aroma, impelling him to heights of rapture in unfettered leaps as he hopped among the hearty plants.

He abruptly halted these festivities when the thought of time surfaced. A great sigh descended upon him as he dropped to his knees. "I am back to my own universe. How I do love thee." And he raised himself up, weeping passionately, and began the long walk home.

* * * * *

The world seemed a naked place to him now, stripped of the ornamental and glittering veils that shielded its true nature from its inhabitants.

He stopped, for he could discern a faraway choir of birds as they trekked across the high vault of celestial heaven. He searched the sky and saw nothing. He closed his eyes and instinctively stretched his arms toward the horizon, with his hands, palms open, probing the warm air. He felt something, a shape, a density, a ripple in the breeze, an anomaly in the texture and composition of the atmosphere. These patterns moved slowly, and his hands followed as he felt the wavelike motions of the shapes swoop and dive and soar. These emanations began to spread into his body in a flowing and humming pulse, and he felt that he was in rhythm and rhyme with its essence and could communicate to it; and so he began a whistle born from a new, innate ability to translate the songs that had been approaching, and he felt this music of the birds swim through the air as he caressed the images with his large hands. The shapes veered from their course, and he felt as if he could guide them to himself, as if the sky was a sea of interconnecting senses and energies that he had only to touch to signal another living thing. It was like plucking the strings of an exquisite harp in order to achieve sound.

He could feel the objects draw nearer, and soon they were close to him; and as he opened his emerald-colored eyes, behold, a flock of snow-white birds alighted atop his out-stretched arms, twittering and fluttering about even as he sang his unique song of understanding and welcome. His head fell back as he looked up into the clouds; with tears in his eyes, his voice was full of pathos as he whispered, "What am I?"

He continued walking toward home, observing the natural foliage with great curiosity; for, it seemed to him, their hues deepened in quality, and were mixed with hitherto unknown colors, and these colors began to grow in intensity, sprouting new identities with every passing moment, encircling him in a cascading and spiraling fashion, imparting great pleasure to his senses. He saw the plants vibrate and blossom into a multitudinous layer of purple, many shades deep, covered with a surface green that boasted light and dark and jade to its admirer; and then a halo of violet sprung about the petals, reaching around the surface in a gushing shower of misty columns. He looked about himself and saw that all the forest had begun to transcend its previous attire. It was as if, he thought, a master painter had mixed in all the colors of the rainbow and poured it on every tree and bush and grass, brightening each segment with an element of polish and splendor.

He could taste the ripe fumes of this bursting aroma form about his flaring nostrils, and felt the pale ebb of humanity stir within him, leading him past this gentle hymn, this tranquil melody, which beckoned him to stay. He fell away, averting his eyes, and began to run through the forest until he came to a clearing and fell to his knees in exhaustion. "Is this a new world," he thought, "or am I a new creature?" He picked himself up and sighted his home, which was some half-mile in the distance.

He felt a sudden compulsion to close his eyes as he began the trek. He turned around in a full circle, bowed his head, raised it, and waved his hands about. He felt images being extracted from the landscape, absorbed into his mind, translated and stored. He began to walk, and he did not stumble nor fall, nor strike an obstacle, for his mind wove a safe path, one that was winding and turning and narrow, which he navigated smoothly and steadily and easily.

His eyes opened. There sat his home.

"Rymalone."

He saw nothing, yet heard his name spoken in a strained voice.

"Rymalone, my love, I need you."

It was his wife, he knew, but she was not outside.

He opened the door.

There she lay, on the floor, writhing in a furious eruption of excruciating pain. "Rymalone, my darling, you came back," she whispered, her eyes still closed, her slender body, turned away from him, drenched in a noxious sweat.

"Joelene," he spoke softly, and upon gently caressing her wet, auburn hair, "I am here, darling."

She clasped his hands as he knelt at her side.

He felt a split, a tear in the harmonic wave in his mind, as if he could feel the sensations of pain that her tormented body emitted. He placed his right hand upon her neck, and immediately a message of disorientation, a flurry of skewed messages and jumbled impulses cried out to him. As he passed his fingers over every region of her body, he felt a destroying presence in one area, and in another, a rhythmic throb of energy that sang health to him. He let his hand dwell on the area where the agony was magnified, and let his mind wander.

There was a vile harvest thriving in her neck, a mass of infection that was sending out its ravenous tentacles to consume adjoining cells. He acknowledged its existence, felt its singular roar and arrogant hiss, and so let his other hand move across her back to feel the strength of her immune system; yet her forces signaled feebleness and timidity, impelling him to move both of his hands to her neck.

He closed his eyes and felt a prodigious flare of unmitigated strength about his body, and he summoned it to come forth and pour out its soothing and healing hand to quench this consuming fire of decay and rust.

His hands bled life.

He directed the power into her disease, ushered in recruits, deployed defenses, caught escaping prisoners; and when the battle was won, he felt exhausted.

She sat up and stared deeply into his eyes. Her voice was unsure and shaking with wonderment. "You were gone so long, my love," she whispered, and as she clasped her hands, she seemed to begin to comprehend what had occurred. "It is over. I am as I once was," she murmured, bewildered, her visage lit by the shock of profound discovery, "and though I hoped and prayed, I did not expect it now; but what have I done, why now?" And she beheld him as he was, now, for the first time. "It is thee."

He told her everything about the Source.

"I hold an ambitious fury within me," he continued, "desirous to touch and feel and hear and see and smell all things anew; and by doing such acts, I grow, as a young and eager flower grows, stretching its supple and willowy body toward the warm, yellow sun." He put his right hand upon her face and gently stroked it. "I feel your soft and downy skin; and yet, I feel its texture, its unique composition, as if all its cells can be read by my hand." He stood up and walked over to a vase full of roses of many colors, easily pulled them out, and walked back to her, all the while feeling the essence of the petals. He gave them to her, and then he closed his eyes. "Give one to me." She assented, and he held the rose and caressed the softy, velvety petals with his thick, long fingers. "Yellow."

She gasped.

"Hand them to me," he continued. He felt all of them, and identified each one by its dominant color, and then said, "The world is no longer a mass of faceless objects that lie in anonymity. It is as if," and here he seemed to drift away from her, "I am being drawn, atom by atom, into a greater world, another universe, inhabited by Nature and unseen by humanity. Though I desire its sensuous touch, I have begun to fear that I might transcend your world." He looked at her and she could see his sudden cognizance of her. His countenance was grim. "Mrs. Browning."

She clutched his hands. "Her cancer; oh, Rymalone, is it possible?"

* * * * *

Charlotte Browning lay in a weeping torrent of agony. Her knotted and arthritic hands shook; her legs, swollen and discolored, had a great expanse of bulging tumors growing out of them; death, like the tidal wave of heat in summer, was soon to come.

Rymalone and Joelene walked in and smelled the moisture and rot of foul disease.

"Mrs. Browning," Joelene said tenderly, "it is Joelene and Rymalone."

Charlotte put out her twisted clump of withered fingers and clasped Joelene's hands. She whispered their names.

He knelt beside her as she lay on the old gray sofa with the lopsided cushion and ripped upholstery, and he looked into eyes consumed with a nauseated desire for calm and peace. "Do you desire death?" he asked solemnly.

He lips trembled. "No," she whispered, "I want life so that I might be of benefit to others. I want death only if it is the will of God."

He shook his head. "Why?"

"My life," she murmured, and a violent convulsion chewed her voice into bits of hot shrapnel, "is unfulfilled."

"What would you do?" asked Joelene, still clutching the old woman's sweaty hands.

Tears visited her pale mask. "Help the poor, bring succor to the sick and dying." She stared deeply into her eyes. "I want to live only to serve God; to die is selfishness."

He felt a secret warmth of decency engorge his heart. "It shall be done," he thought, and placed his hands upon her emaciated legs.

The tumors dispersed like butter melting on a rock in the burning noonday sun.

He was spent when he came back into his home, for Charlotte's regeneration had taken ten minutes, and he felt as if he had fought a long battle with a mighty lion. He drained a large glass of fresh, cool spring water, fell to rest, woke up some four hours later, and decided to walk into town.

The long journey through the forest, far away from the Source, swept his mind into another place, for he began to see all creatures, great and small, all plants, green and brown, all decay, all rocks, all soil, all sunlit beams and wispy hazes and dappled shadows not as separate entities but as assuming the role of a symmetrical unity, a fusion of separate parts into a single species with many shapes and forms and sizes.

He was frightened, and did not understand.

He stood now, with eyes closed and hands outstretched, at the end of the dirt path, ingesting the commotion of civilization in the distance. There were too many images and smells and noises and jumbled, rambling clutter that diffused across a vast landscape. He withdrew his abilities and marched onward.

There was a shopping center directly in front of him, and he stood before the sloppy architecture, his swarthy countenance grim. "This is not good," he mused, "this is not Nature, not life, not coherent," and he closed his eyes to smell the fine particles of glamorous scents floating about. The pollution, however, invaded his nostrils and he swiftly covered his nose, and then waited, relaxed, released his hands, and began again.

A floating iceberg of odors crashed down upon him, and he could not decipher their meaning or origin. A multifarious army of aromas sank into his brain, and he began to concentrate on one only, and in so doing, gave it an authentic autograph that liberated it from the others: donuts.

The gooey and sumptuous divinity of the chewy, fluffy, delicate dough, immersed in a startling bath of poisonous fat and drenched in various dress of sugary delights, struck him. There were glazed donuts and maple-frosted ones and chocolate-crème-filled and delicious mounds of glorious gobs of sweet and rich jelly-filled donuts, all filling his senses and forming a distinct line, a formation through the air that implored him to its perfumed, scented lair.

He opened his eyes and saw that the donut shop was down the street some two hundred yards. A siren full of perplexity hit him as his eyes wandered about the stores and scattered businesses. He closed his eyes again, relaxed, waited, and dissected another smell from the aggressive attack bombing his olfactory organ. This time the sizzling aroma of cooking, spicy chicken swept down upon him. This was to his left and some forty yards away. And so it began, the shearing of this bulging sinew of smell until he could locate and follow any particular one. He would walk with his head down so as not to attract attention, navigating his path throughout the city based solely on the emissions of smell from businesses that harbored food products. If he wished to find the bookstore, which he knew to be next to the delicatessen, he had only to fix on that restaurant's unique beam of savory delights and follow it; and though he was some two hundred yards away from the deli when he started, nonetheless, he arrived on target.

He soon tired of this game and decided to visit the local bakery so as to purchase a loaf of fresh, warm sourdough bread.

He stood, eyes closed, with a silly grin on his face, inhaling deeply for twenty minutes, unaware of the stares of customers, unconscious of the world, until the manager spoke to him and finally nudged his arm. Rymalone looked about, bewildered, until realization fluttered down to him and he gathered himself, bought a loaf, and exited the store, hurrying along, his head and thick, brown, curly hair hanging forward, his handsome visage aglow with embarrassment and wonder.

He sat on the park bench and sucked on the yellow-whitish dough, cherished its buttery texture, worshipped its pleasing smell, swooned over its blessed taste; thirty minutes hence and he had devoured only one slice of it. He decided, on a whim, to share his treasure. Looking about and seeing no one, he waved his right hand and a flock of brown sparrows flew to the verdant grass before him. "Here, my friends," he said, lovingly, "perhaps you can appreciate this fine meal," and as he fed them, a smile appeared upon his face, for he was happy.

And so it was that Rymalone became enthralled in the vitality and exquisite excellence of his heightened senses, and he journeyed into the forest and then into town every day for two weeks, sampling the quality and charm of its surroundings much as a baby explores the world once it can crawl.

But, alas, Joelene became a distant participant in his union with his new world, as he was so absorbed in this new species of heightened senses and the exquisite delights he experienced, that he would not listen to her pleas to aid those in physical distress.

On the fifteenth day of his holy pilgrimage into the city, he decided, at nine o'clock in the a.m., to stop by the college library to find a book on preparing fine foods.

At nine o'clock that same night, after the librarian had signaled the people, by turning the lights off and on, that departure time was nigh, she came upon a man hidden from view by a tower of books, eight rows in all, each on a different subject.

All things relating to physics were to the far left; and going to his right, there were topics on chemistry, astronomy, molecular biology, geology, mathematics, history, philosophy, psychology, anthropology, and religion. There was one book sitting by itself, abandoned, it seemed, and looked down upon by the other haughty works: one on gourmet cooking.

There was an extreme commotion of energy radiating about him, she noticed, for he turned the pages of his book with an urgent fury to devour its contents; sometimes he would stop for a moment, his face lost in a deep frown, until he turned the pages back and read another passage, impelling him to return to the other page and then slap his hand upon the table in triumph, letting out a controlled "Ha!" while his animated face roared with intense pleasure. She spied his swift processions through the texts and saw the quizzical expression on his face pass to understanding with a rapidity that increased with time.

"Excuse me, sir, but we are closing now," she finally said, politely.

He had no need to look up. "Do not worry about me," he returned, almost in a state of agitation, while waving his right hand about as if to signify the authority and righteousness in his words.

She waited for him to continue, but he did not. "Sir," she restated, her words now tipped with an air of power, "all the people in the library, except library personnel, must leave. It is closing time."

There occurred to him, at that very moment, a most singular kind of pulsing hum in his mind, which was pushed out and away into the void to transmute any extraneous noise into meaningless tones; this cleaning seemed to affect him in a profound manner, for he now lost cognizance of the human voice directed at him, which was now perceived as a throbbing, painful emittance that would not die. Thus, it was necessary to move it away.

He raised his hand and felt the current of the voice, its weak sound waves crashing against him like a dying ember, and he pushed it back to its source with the noise from his mind, driving the essence of its nature into her brain to sit and sputter and spin in dull and confusing waves. She began to tremble and mumble in horror, her mind rebelling against such trespasses. This eerie state, driven so unmercifully into her mind, caused her to weep, as a child weeps when he is left alone in the dark.

A faint and shriveled echo of pain trickled into his mind.

He looked up and beheld a face bound by hopelessness and fear, and this caused him to cease his control over her. She stood as one does who is lifted suddenly from the looting and raping of a gory nightmare.

She felt the wetness upon her warm cheeks, and she turned in shame, for she did not know how this had come to be.

A clawing sensation, wedded to an eagerness for calm, faded away from him as he stood. "What have I done?" he mumbled to himself. "What have I allowed myself to do?" And he began to panic, ushering in desperation to flee and submerge himself far away from civilization.

He held out his arms as he walked toward her. His voice was delicate and soft. "Forgive me," he whispered, and he stood in front of her, his hands on hers. "Can I help in any way? Please…"

Her old hands, her trembling, weak hands grasped his as she spoke in a voice full of forlornness. "I should not be here. I should have retired long ago. I am so old and full of pride," and she looked into his deep-set, luminous eyes, "and I am going to die soon."

His hands were drawn to a region of her head that created, to him, a mask of death, originating from a large mass of tumors beyond the reach of lasers and surgery, and he suddenly appraised his life of late as imperious and self-absorbed; Joelene, he thought, you were right—why have I not turned my gaze to those in need?

When he resurfaced from the stale and polluted environment of the library, he thrust his head out into the cool, fresh breeze that swept his sweating and weakened form. He inhaled with eyes closed and mouth open, panting strongly, his body quivering from exhaustion. He slid down the stone steps, holding onto the top portion of the cement wall, and upon reaching the sidewalk, halted for a moment and inhaled deeply. He could feel the rich oxygen being sucked into his lungs, and his mind sought to extract it in greater quantities; and so he breathed in mighty heaves, devouring concentrated gulps of it until he felt alive, invigorated, dynamic, addicted to its regenerative powers as he moved on. A man, coming from the opposite direction, passed by him; and at that very moment the man began to choke and gasp, and then it passed. This man looked around, his hands still at his throbbing, reddening throat, and all he could see was the curious figure who continued to run down the street at an incredible speed.

* * * * *

A scar of contempt formed across the man's large, white face as he slowly drifted toward the busy boulevard, and as he came to rest on the sidewalk, he viewed the diverse life about him.

"Why are these people alive? Why do they deserve to live?" he mused. "What have they done but bring misery and destruction to the world? If only they could think for a moment and see what they are, what they have brought upon innocent people," but then he gestured about himself; "oh, bah! It's all foolishness. Look at them, I say, look at the poor idiots! They blubber along like children lost in the dark!"

Within him disgust mounted a messenger fleet of foot, and broke, with its ensuing message, upon his burning countenance, lying comfortably atop well-bred contempt. "Egad," he shouted in his furious thoughts as his eyes beheld a woman of tremendous proportions, "is she alive? Does she think? How can she attain such a monumental hulk? She certainly must be dedicated, like a perpetual factory, to shoveling great masses of food into her gaping mouth with an assiduousness unsurpassed! Incredible!" He watched in horror as the woman stopped to buy a triple-decker chocolate ice cream cone. "She could have health, yet she throws it all away; and when she has her inevitable heart attack—perhaps at this very moment, her poor pump is about to expire in anticipation of this lethal con-glomeration of dead foodstuff—she will be rolled to the hospi-tal, and in so doing, cause our insurance rates to soar." Outrage courted him until it blew up into a haughty rage. "And for what, I say?—for flagrant stupidity!" His animated visage drew back in utter disbelief as she commenced to hand an ice cream to her cherubic son. "The fiend, she corrupts innocent minds, too," he shouted, and people walking by him looked about, expecting to see such a person; "curse you, you willing monument to ignorance," and he threw up his arms and then pointed an outstretched hand toward her. He soon found that he was forced to look elsewhere, so great was his displeasure and his feeling of helplessness.

"People, left to think and act on their own, would cor-rupt a flower," he reasoned. "They work, they copulate, they eat, they play, they excrete waste," and then he shouted in his mind with great emphasis, "and then they eat and copulate and work again; good night! It's an absurd cycle for morons, imbeciles, and idiots! They are a plague upon our world; it would be better if they were as the plants—rooted in sub-mission—but as they are, people are merely animals with the ability to communicate through oral and written language, and not very adept, at that!" A malicious sneer crawled across his meaty face. "Hobbs was wrong: it doesn't matter if the political community exists, for people are too exceptionally ignorant to take advantage, so: the life of man is still solitary, poor, nasty, brutish, and short—and if it isn't, it should be! And to think they think themselves superior to Nature—bah!" and here he gesticulated against the world, in general, with a wide sweep of his long-sleeved arms. He watched, stone-faced, as the woman and son entered into their car. "That poor automobile," he whispered; "if it could speak, it would most certainly howl in protest." He exhaled long and hard and looked away again. He then journeyed forth across the street to continue his shopping. "Were all the human race a bug, and my foot raised above it; this is my fondest desire."

* * * * *

The ice cream was so absurdly flavorful, so tantalizing and exploding with such sweet scents in her mouth, so exquisite in its rich and thick, fatty, sugary taste, that the woman wondered, at that delicious moment in time, why she did not consume such food all the day long, and then, upon further reflection, she admitted that she did.

She then stepped, with great emphasis, upon the gas pedal.

As the luscious, smooth mixture of delectable cream slid down her hot throat, she was committed, by lust, to sustain such intense pleasure, and perhaps, if it were possible, to heighten it; this meant, naturally, that she must perpetuate a rhythmic motion, excelling in eye to hand coordination, which allowed a continuous licking of the syrupy dessert.

The divine mistress to her belly began to slip away from her messy fingers, and she followed its path, instantaneously, with outstretched arms and imploring eyes and bending head, as it soared toward the dusty carpet of the old Chevrolet. It was then that a most unusual event occurred, one that prompted her to halt all operations.

There came a dull, squishing, aching thud to her ears, and her bewildered look soon turned to a frantic desire to know what had transpired.

The air became drenched in an acrid odor, swamped in a rancid pulp that crashed into her flaring nostrils and raged like lightning throughout her as she looked upon the man pinned under the back wheels of her vehicle.

Issuing forth a mighty howl, she quickly bent down behind the car, took the chrome rear bumper into her fat and chocolate-covered hands, and proceeded, with little effort, to lift it up and over several feet so as to free the man completely.

But, alas, he was dead already, and having deduced this very fact from a thorough and maddening check for his pulse, she, in the midst of the growing mass of citizen gawkers, began to crumble, in every way imaginable.

Her countenance took on a reddish glow as her corpulent cheeks trembled and her body quaked. "Foolish woman," she screamed, and she was now oblivious of any company, or of her boy, who sat in a murky fog in the backseat of the car, "don't you ever think," and she pounded her fists against her large head, pummeling it with such ferocity that the crowd, as if a single organism, reeled back in shock and dread. "No more," she shouted, and stomped her feet, "no more, you foolish and selfish woman," and she closed her mouth and eyes tightly, her arms half-bent outward from her side. The crowd, like a spider on a web, felt a horrific vibration, and pushed further away even as she achieved the desired result.

She fell, quite simply, dead, face forward upon the victim, who lay upon his back.

It was then that a stranger approached the fallen combatants, a man who possessed a countenance of great equanimity and certitude. His voice was a cool draft in the minds of the frightened people.

"They are not dead; they are merely asleep," he said to himself, looking at the two bodies with his head askew; and he bent down to the woman, and placed his hands upon her heart; and behold, she awoke, and presently sat up, much to the amazement of the hushed crowd.

"Perhaps the woman," an old man declared, "but not the man, for he is dead for sure."

The stranger answered the old man, his eyes still drawn toward the wounds of the downed person, "Have you examined him?"

Silence fell like soft petals in a rain forest.

And behold, upon the stranger laying his hands upon the dead man's chest, the man then opened his eyes, coughed loudly and sat up. The crowd collapsed in terror and stupefaction, many of them running to and fro; others, unthinking, began to mumble and turn away; and still others stayed, desirous to know the truth.

The police and paramedics came upon the scene with great alacrity, and such commotion allowed Rymalone to escape the attention once heaped upon him; he ran swiftly—and even though he focused on the rapid evacuation and separation of oxygen from the atmosphere, thus filling his burning lungs with generous amounts of it—he labored still as he passed people who clutched at their throats in panic.

He could feel his internal physiology waning, and this fact propelled him to trek into the forest, moving at a swift, yet stumbling pace.

His mind, savaged by this virulent rupture deep in his tissues and organs, spoke of imminent death. He had to return to this Womb, to feel Her comforting presence, to nourish himself on Her immense powers so that he might yet live.

The woods were soaked in a quiescent harvest of solemn beauty and golden sunshine plunging all about him as he fell before the Source, prostrate, gasping, weak, close to death.

His face lay nestled in a sweet clump of moist leaves and fresh, fertile soil that was bursting with the taste of life and promise of seed and rebirth, cuddling him softly as he crawled to the edge of the opening. If he looked, if he beheld its swirling, ebony vapors, he would be taken. He hesitated.

"Again," he cried aloud, "again!" and as he desperately sought to inhale and extract the precious element of oxygen from the air, yet again and again he failed. He thrust his hands into the grainy, brown dirt and, lying upon his back, summoned pure intellect to pursue this matter until it chewed it into a million fragments.

His mind united with his body and he felt a flow of energy surge throughout him, and he felt his desire for precious oxygen subside as his breathing slowed and his body relaxed. Fresh breath floated within him—sweet, silent, deep and slow, in long pauses, quite blissful and powerful. He began to panic, then, because he would inhale and exhale over and again, but then this rhythm would abruptly halt; yet he felt vigorous and dynamic. The seconds elapsed and he was presented with a flowing trill of peace and harmony buzzing in his mind. Then, after twenty seconds, a slow and powerful breath occurred, which reached far down to inject its precious jewel deep within his starving tissues; and then his exhale came, sweeping up the waste and expelling this toxic cargo in copious amounts, and in so doing he was purified, cleansing him of all decay and rot and disease that came with mortality.

His heart slowed to twelve beats a minute.

After Rymalone had departed from the rim of the Source, a man, who had been surreptitiously tucked away behind a cluster of Douglas fir trees, moved forward to the curious gap in the forest floor. "The man saves my life from that horrible behemoth who should never again see the light of day—bah! The man gives me life, and then he stumbles to this strange..." Yet Lewis Ferris did not finish his sentence, for his gaze was drawn into the pit with such intensity to explore its internal working that he stood, frozen, mesmerized, his youthful mind loosening its grip upon his physical movements.

In an imperceptible movement forward, he simply was no longer on the ground but falling into the circular hole, his countenance embalmed in a shock of outrage.

* * * * *

It was near dawn, and Rymalone lay upon his bed and felt the rush of his environment climb up to him and invite itself in; and he did not deter such efforts, for their delicious essence enthralled him without consuming him.

Joelene came into his room, holding a newspaper in her hand, and she sat beside him. Her voice was full of a reserved joy. "Scientists have confirmed the Cold Fusion Theory you sent to the *Times*," and she held up the newspaper, and the headlines read, "Cold Fusion Now!" She smiled, though she wasn't sure why. "And they are researching your theory on eradicating nuclear waste through natural processes, increasing food production tenfold without disturbing the ecosystem, and curing all kinds of cancers."

He was looking out of the wooden-framed window when he spoke, his voice melancholy, "I composed a symphony this morning," and he looked at her suddenly, "well, in my head, actually," he gestured with his hands, and then looked outside again to the subtle dance of the radiant beams of sunshine, and the magical frolic of the tiny masters of Nature as they scurried about in their perpetual pursuit of food. "I'm thinking about submitting it to the local philharmonic." He sighed heavily. "This is music that is in perfect synchronization and rhythm with the pulses of the human body, yet," a sibilant hiss poured forth from his lips, and he soon turned his head to meet her gaze, "I'm afraid," he stated, his voice desolate and tortured, "to leave this sanctuary." He closed his eyes. "If I see pain and suffering, I must, by my nature, succor the ailing person; yet, in so doing, I pull further away from you and closer," and here he looked out into the forest, "to the Source. What will become of me if this continues…" He paused, looking down as he moved his hand back and forth in front of himself, and then declared, in a somber voice, "I just read the imprints of the newspaper—how can you live with someone who can do that? What about tomorrow?"

She held him then, and her pious tears flowed without restraint. "Whatever happens, my darling," she whispered, "we shall always be one; indivisible, equal and united together."

At that very moment, in a small clearing between a gathering of mighty Canyon Live Oak trees, an opening in the ground appeared, circular in shape, some six feet in diameter, and emitting no light or smell or sound. A swirl, a ballet of spongy, moist, fluffy grass enveloped the rip of this gap, a verdant sea stretching out in all directions for several yards. In the air there was the fragrance of the conifers and their ripe, succulent sap, and the scent of the tender blossoms and their sensuous aroma.

The smell of life and natural processes of birth and death and rebirth seemed to reach a frenzy as a fertilized egg was ejected from the abyss in a silent blast and came to rest upon the thick blanket of flora; immediately, it began to grow, and as it did so, it acquired all the characteristics of its surroundings: the power, the abilities, and the processes of the secret lives of the forest; their functions, their insights, their marvels were transformed into this egg, as it increased in size minute by minute; soon, it was obvious that a human figure was being sculpted, but there were a multitude of other forms that were now part of it; yes, there were two arms and legs, but then: the arms were vibrant green and flowing with the green juice of plant life, chlorophyll, and then the legs were brown, as thick as corrugated tree trunks; arms like the magnificent spread of the bald eagle; legs now as supple and sinewy as the swift cheetah; arms now like the long, flowing River Nile, legs now like a swirling waterfall; and his body: now like a Tyrannosaurus rex, like a mighty typhoon, like a fiery volcano, bursting with unbound energy and vigor and power—like a hurricane, a raging conflagration, a huge earthquake; and his head: human, fire, ice, wind; his eyes: hawk eyes, eyes of glittering diamonds, eyes as pure as the deepest crystalline-opal sea; and his hair: like heaps of translucent snow, like the hearty green pastures, like the wispy cumulus clouds; and he grew, and grew, until he was fully mature, and taller than the tallest treetops; and lo, he gazed about himself in wild wonder, and his eyes, blazing like molten rubies, widened, and he held up his head and beheld the deep, azure sky, and howled, so that all the forest stretched out their subservient forms to him, and those who could, bowed; and those who could, knelt; and those who could, lay.

He looked about the land, and decided he should, for a while, lower himself to the physical size and appearance of his former species; and so, with a thought, he was soon his original height, but natural still; and as he walked, he adorned himself in the luscious finery of his environs; and then, feeling weary, he stuck his feet into the luxurious soil, and felt the invigorating energy of life course through him. "I and Nature, thee and me; we are one," he thought.

Immediately, with shock and restraint as his new companions, he began to fondle the inhabitants of the woods, slowly at first, and hesitantly; upon the realization that indeed they were as they seemed, he unhooked the lock upon his emotions and began to roll and tumble and crawl about, all the while laughing and crying and shouting great proclamations of joy.

* * * * *

When Lewis Ferris completed his adulation of Nature, he began to walk in the direction of the city; but his mind, having experienced a shift in sensory abilities, halted the mechanical motion of his body. His blue eyes blurred, for the images they beheld were being processed too quickly and he could not discern the parade of objects and their shapes and sizes and dimension and color. He became frightened, and began to whimper as he fell to his knees. "My sight," he wailed, "on the eve of destruction! May it never be! My eyes are the sun in a world veiled by darkness!" He was astounded by such eloquent speech, and as he wiped the tears from his black orbs, his vision adjusted to a world hitherto unknown to him.

Upon looking up into the patches of light streaking down between the spaces in the trees, he beheld a radiant display of violet seeping into the landscape; yet, it was not alone, for beside it, in a lighter shade, was indigo, and next to this lay blue, then green, yellow, orange and red. His mind stumbled for a moment in analysis of this phenomenon. "A rainbow," he mused, "of course, but unlike any rainbow I have encountered," and here he let his vision wander about this fabulous new garden of delights, "for it radiates everywhere." He put up his hands to feel it, and behold, it moved, seeping back into pure, white light. He fell backward at this reaction, and when he lowered his hands, the rainbow again appeared.

He then beheld fleeting wisps of thermal energy floating about him, streaking everywhere in a thick horde. "Some kind of cosmic radiation," he thought, still incredulous.

His eyes were diverted to a mass of loosely flowing red lines that struck the rocks and bushes and plants in a perpetual, shifting shower, which gently flowed in a wave-like motion that seemed to move like swaying trees. The air smelled like the charged breeze of an electrified storm, and he moved toward eerie, oscillating bands of glowing waves. As the red lines bathed him in their fiery light, they began to move about him in a mighty vortex, feeding into him their power and essence, and he could hear their message, feel their song leaping and flying through his mind—for they spoke the wave language of their master, of radio and television. But the rapidity with which the descent of the voluminous messages crashed into him was too great, forcing him to hold up his arms to shield himself from its force as he stepped back into the comfort of a towering tree. "Egad!" he shouted. "To live in that maelstrom for a moment longer would be death!" And he shook himself, as if to undress the impact of the previous event. But then a curious thought occurred to him. "Yet," and his urging voice ebbed, "to absorb such a transcendent event into one's mind and process it as one does an innocent ray of sunshine! Ah!" and he thrust himself out into the hail of scarlet-colored flowing patterns, hurling his arms about as his mind sought to ease the onslaught of information pouring into his brain cells; and he began to gambol about, screaming incoherent things, holding tight his ears, shouting, yelping in terror, strangling on the welling tide of news until at last his hands fell from his ears and he stood there with a look of victory emblazoned upon his shining visage.

He fell to his knees upon the deep mush of the soil, his lips pulled back in glee, his eyes glowing with rapture; and his voice, captured by revelations unknown to Mankind, produced a commanding pitch of absolute certitude. "Power," bubbled from his widening mouth, as if, at that precise moment, he sought to capture its very essence. "I am alive," he suddenly shouted, "and the world shall know my name."

The perspiration of the night air soaked his glistening body as he galloped at speeds beyond the capacity of even extraordinary men. Upon reaching the end of the forest, he stopped, and not liking the loud and accelerated pounding of his heart, he looked inside himself and quieted it with the stroke of his slender fingers upon his heaving chest. Though his heart beat slower, he could still hear it contracting and resting, pumping blood through his circulatory system—and although he heard the blood rushing through arteries and veins, he thought nothing of it, and continued onward, looking upon the world as if he were a newborn child.

In the distance there came a faint sound, a quivering kind of gibbering, a polluted squadron of human voices smeared into a fused and tangled blob that he could not separate for clarity. He thought that perhaps a festival of some kind was happening, for the voices of the attendants, to him, were so boisterous and rapid that the range of emotion kept the emitted sound in a continuous clamor. Yet, his frustration, evidenced by his knit brows and pursed lips, mounted, for he saw nothing to quench his desire to see the source of the noise. "Miles," he declared, "I cannot see a thing for miles, and yet," he commanded, "I hear aplenty; why, it's quite maddening." Thus, impelled by a burning desire to know, he commenced to running, at a speed slightly faster than ever before.

His senses seemed to inhale the obstacles that Nature had placed before him, and to sort them out in a rather facile manner, at the same moment plotting a safe and sure course through the entanglements of the dense foliage. Presently, he came upon a carnival, which provoked no little wrath in him, for in his private ponderings, he saw a collection of weak and tragic lost souls plodding about in a profound stupor, accumulating more lost time to heave upon the rest of their lost lives. He stopped at the periphery of the event, very aware of the increased malignancy of confusion of noise bounding about his brain. "The peasant rogues," he said, washing them clean in his mind, "have they no other union than with sloth and degradation?" Yet, the massive web of noise usurped his rages, and he fell to his knees, his hands covering his burning ears, his eyes intent upon finding the source of this malady. The revelation poured upon him quickly, and his anger increased when a kindly old man approached him.

"Sir," the old gentleman began, "may I assist you in any way? Is there anything wrong?" and then gasped when he beheld the multifarious hues of Nature's skin that the stranger wore.

Yet, this voice was merely another jumbled message in a huge ball of compacted messages, and one that seemed to ring louder and more vexing than the others. He could feel the compression waves, produced by the man's utterance of speech, strike his face, smoothing over his contorted flesh. He held up his hand when the man spoke again, and he caught the sound waves in his left hand, and feeling its substance, pushed it back to the old man, who felt a violent flood of gushing air pound against his aching head. The old man attempted to speak, yet nothing came out, and his mind took to panic, causing him to wander away in a confused state.

Lewis focused his mind on one section of the carnival, where, one hundred yards away, the merry-go-round was being operated. Slowly, the childish laughter and voices of its inhabitants began to grow distinct to him, then lower in decibels, until he could pull out the voice of a small, red-haired child who was imploring her mother for another ride. He heard it all, as if they were in a room with him, speaking slowly and carefully. He looked round to another spot. There, a carnival man was attempting to coax a young couple into playing at his game booth for a prize. Lewis blocked the hundreds of others voices out, or, rather, adjusted their volume downward, while sharpening the dialogue of the three at the booth.

Night had hoisted its black and silken cloak upon them, giving aid to those who thrived on its sable fog for stealth and anonymity. Lewis gazed to his left and saw a teenage boy and girl sneak out into the forest for a quick rendezvous with the delights of romance.

A young mother came by, shouting out the name of her male child, the same boy guilty of the covert operation in the woods.

Lewis concentrated upon the couple and spoke, feeling his voice transported across the distance in a singular and specially crafted trumpet that was able to deliver his message at their precise spot. "Young man," he shouted, not near his person, but only upon them, "come back to your mother, for she seeks you even now." The frightened look upon their faces amused him; and indeed, they obeyed this mysterious command, running back with great haste to the bright lights of the festival.

And yet, he forgot their adventure, for he felt something else anew; he smelled their fear, like one smells a fresh rose covered with morning dew or a newly baked rye bread; he felt their pitiful plight, their human frailty excrete itself into the air, and he wondered why he had never smelled something so obvious and so common before. "It is such an ostensible and irreversible part of their being, it is a wonder that I have not been fouled by its malodorous chemical my entire life!"

There was an old-fashioned outdoor movie screen once used in drive-ins, and when he happened to look at it, he shook his head and blinked, but when he saw it again, there was a noticeable interruption of the rapid succession of images in a single frame that combined to give the viewer a clear, unbroken, fluid image, for now his eyes beheld the dark, blank frame in between; and then, as his vision adjusted, all of the frames slowed and it was as if he were merely looking at a giant cartoon flip-book; he had to turn away, bewildered even more.

He then navigated his way home with both eyes closed, and immediately went to bed.

He woke up that night with terror at his side, for he felt the natural processes of his body in a magnified and vivid expression of their enthusiasm toward function. His heart contracted and pushed the blood into his body, and he heard the gushing pound of the organ, the swish of the blood as it raced on its way; then, a pause would come, and the process would repeat, but he could not separate his senses from this sound. He heard the coursing of the blood rushing swiftly through his veins and arteries as if his ear was inside his body, inside an enclosed structure and absorbing all the noises and echoes from all areas of his anatomy.

He felt his tingling and clammy skin, drenched in perspiration, sliding against black bedsheets, and he felt as if his nose and eyes and ears were pressing against every inch of the sheet that touched his hypersensitive skin.

At that very moment, he felt as if his body was in a cocoon as his mind was carried through a maddening journey of sounds and smells and sight and touch and taste that were no longer confined to only one sense each—as each sense now became a single unit, a living, functioning organism that synergistically heightened his powers to become one sense, the consummate sense, a movable tyrant full of a bloat of self-glory and avarice, sucking all of his energies until it completed its metamorphosis.

Lewis began screaming and howling as his mind took in the voices of the people who seemed to surround him, and he heard their external clamoring and yammering, upon which his squirming brain fed, as he could not separate them and isolate them and bury them, either by ones or twos or threes, or in any way, shape or form, for they were as voices ricocheting in his head like bullets perpetually fired in a sealed, steel cave.

And then he commenced, in his mind, to dig a wound so vast and deep that he might, with all the problems of his world, crawl into it and become undiscovered.

For it was then he felt them all over his body, all of them squiggling and squatting and jumping and laughing at him because now he understood, and they knew it—it was the microbes, all of them; the infinitesimal monsters, the germs and bugs so extraordinarily and wonderfully fashioned so as not to be detected by the ordinary mind. Yet, his extraordinary mind felt them on every portion of his skin, felt their creep and vicious caress over his pores and follicles.

His skin was alive.

All of these sensations transpired within a short duration, and since he could not master these new abilities swiftly enough, he fled into a dark, warm sanctuary inside his head until it all went away; even as his body shook and his mouth roared hideous atrocities at seemingly invisible invaders; even as his hand swept all over and about his body in gushing massive rips and tears and pulls and punches; even as the slimy, boiling sweat poured out like blood; and even as his body, in a closed-up, crunched-up position, with legs drawn in, on the bed, bounced about as his feet pounded in a wild cadence, his mind was tucked gently and happily away from the horror, digesting only those nutrients it needed to survive.

The next day at the public library, clothed for the moment in the garments of those he considered dullards and popinjays, he was noticed by the librarian as he was picking up books and caressing them, one by one, gently at first, then in a manic fury, until he was swiftly running up and down the aisles, touching them and seeming to laugh in response to each one, a laughter derived not from joy but from discovery, the discovery of knowledge and its eventual progeny, power.

"Sir," she said, low, not attempting to attract attention to him, "may I help you?"

At that moment he had just finished spreading his hands over the sections concerning chemistry and physics. He produced a mighty laugh when he turned to her. "Yes," he cried, "more books," and he turned to the next aisle, but instead of running to them, he merely stood and lifted up his hands, as if to receive their complete message in this manner. There was the embryo of unfettered power in his black eyes. "I simply feel the punctuation and dissimilarity of the figures as they rest in the molecular structure of the air, and I assimilate the primitive language into my living, breathing brain."

"Sir," she tried again, ignoring the man's aberrant behavior, "is there a specific book or subject you are interested in?"

His face was now a tapestry upon which he had drawn the vast doorways into absolute knowledge. His voice was explosive and wrapped in the ferment of victory. "Too late," he cried, and then running to the computer, and placing his hands upon it, took all the knowledge from every website in the world, and after he finished, the computer collapsed and melted into a heap of burning black smoke and smoldering ash.

In the forest once more, that dark and brooding night, he allowed himself to reach his full height, and as he gazed about, he could see the minutest detail of anything close, or a little farther away, and then farther away, then miles away, and still farther, hundreds of miles, and then thousands, seeing every person, place and thing in crystal infrared clarity; and sensing the environs there: smells and sounds he experienced as if he were truly standing exactly in their midst; the supple textures he felt as he was touching the objects; the voices he heard as if he were close to the people.

He picked up a large boulder and threw it, and watched in curiosity as it streaked like a burning meteor through the ebony skin of eventide and then landed five thousand miles away as a mere pebble on the exact spot he had aimed—on the roof of a repugnant sausage factory.

"Diversions," he whispered, and his voice thundered.

He felt an abrupt, magnificent bang within his head, and he held his hands on either side at his temples, as he cried, "I remember everything," and the trees were felled, and lay like toothpicks, as if after the terrifying explosion of a mighty volcano.

He remembered all the knowledge he had recently acquired, and it was constantly streaming throughout his swirling mind, all of it at once, and he forgot nothing, not even the slightest, meaningless, most bothersome detail.

"I hear everything," he shouted, his head aimed upward, and the wispy clouds were blown away, and the birds thrown topsy-turvy into the liquid firmament.

He heard everything—all conversations, loud and low, short and long, in every language, comprehending them all, and in every place, noisy or quiet—with crystal clarity, and he remembered them all; and for every new word he heard, it was amassed atop this ever-expanding mountain of words that was now bulging and stretching inside his expanding consciousness.

"I smell everything," he screamed, and his voice echoed like thunder across the land, cracking bridges and windows and buildings.

He smelled everything—all odors of plants, all aromas of food, all perfumed scents that living things give off; and too the scents of products, natural and artificial, all at once, and he could not disentangle his mind from them.

"I feel everything," he howled, in a voice so loud that it swept around the world in reverberating and clamorous echoes, disrupting lives everywhere, and bringing fear and panic to people and animals.

He could feel every kind of texture—rough, smooth, and jagged; and every shape—curved, round, and straight; and every movement—slithering, creaking, and crunching.

"I can taste everything," he grunted, his head bowed now, and the ground split open.

He could taste all odorous molecules in the air: sweet, sour, salty, spicy, rotting, decaying, diseased, smoky, rancid, and ethereal.

"I can see everything," he growled, pounding his large, fisted hands into the earth, and causing a massive quake.

He could see things above the surface of the world, big: buildings, people, mountains, plants, animals, and seas; and small: fungi, insects, bacteria, soil, debris; and as he dug in his bare feet, below himself, too, he saw the outer crust, the mantle, and the inner and outer core.

And for everything that he could see and smell and hear and touch and taste, he saw still: all the detail down to the minutest degree, and all at once, and forgot nothing of it; and so, he beheld the whole wide world in all its splendor and ugliness, its joy and sorrow, its birth and death, and he was more it than himself, and this, he could not abide.

His mind now took in the bounding and leaping locomotion of the full spectrum of electromagnetic radiation: he could see and hear radio waves, every errant and crisscrossing wave and the accompanying noise it carried he heard loud and clear, and it bore into his ear like a hungry tic; he saw and heard microwave, and infrared, he experienced their unique signature; and he heard and saw the visible and ultraviolet, and x-rays, and gamma rays—he experienced the full spectrum, from the lowest frequency, to the highest frequency, and this constant radiation struck his body as if he were immersed in a spectral shower of crepuscular rays.

"Ugh," he shouted, "I must have harmony, I must have peace, I must have sense of self," and he began to transform into a creature hitherto unknown, his body streaked with rainbow-colored veins, his blood at once human, now animal, now plant; his armor-like skin at once human, now animal, now plant; and he began to move, taking huge gulps from the earth with his fanged teeth, and soon finding the silent running spring of purified groundwater, poured its invigorating properties into his gaping mouth, and he grew prodigiously. "Move, I need to move," he cried, and making his way to the ocean, after wrecking homes, roads and buildings, he stepped in, and his body soaked up the briny, frothy soup, filling him with its unique characteristics, whereupon he now began, after moving out farther, to swim inside its murky depths as fast as any sea mammal, and causing tidal waves in his wake.

Presently, he found himself at the bottom of the deepest depths of the ocean, and found hot lava vents, and smashed his way into the four-mile-thick oceanic crust of basalt and iron and magnesium, and absorbed its magnetic field and its unique properties therein; and then smashed his way into the eighteen-hundred-mile-thick, rigid and flowing rock of the mantle, with temperatures ranging from nine hundred degrees to seven thousand degrees Fahrenheit, and absorbed its convection currents, and magnesium and iron and silicon and aluminum, and other properties therein; and then smashed his way into the fourteen-hundred-mile-thick outer core of molten rock, with temperatures from seven thousand degrees to more than nine thousand degrees Fahrenheit, and bathed in it like a newborn, suckling at his mother's nourishing breast, and absorbed the magnetic field, and iron and oxygen, sulfur and nickel alloy, and its other unique properties therein; and so continued on to the nearly one-thousand-mile-thick inner core, with a temperature of nine to thirteen thousand degrees Fahrenheit, as hot as the surface of the sun, and felt the incredible electromagnetic radiation bathing his body in pure, absolute power, and absorbed its iron and oxygen, and sulfur and nickel alloy, and unique properties therein; and he felt alive, dynamic, invincible; but he yearned for more.

"I grow in wealth of power and knowledge, yet the more I have, the more I know I do not have; O, how feeble I am, and how strong I must be," he thought.

And slowly and meticulously he ascended up through the earth, and through the ocean depths, and into the cold air; and lo, the people had been aroused by his disturbing presence, and assembled a great armada to combat him, so that when he appeared, looking like a mighty titan with a body that was a raging mass of lava, water and ice, and plant, animal, and human characteristics, they were very afraid, and began to distribute a barrage of sophisticated weaponry upon this menacing vision.

"So," he laughed, as the projectiles failed to penetrate the electromagnetic field that pulsed about his body like a shining aura, "this is how you welcome your newborn Emperor," and he waved his massive hands, and the metallic ships and jets were easily repulsed and flung far away; and with his breath, out first came fire, then a blast of water, then a sheet of ice; and soon he created a great barrier about himself of fire and ice, where a swirling storm raged within, and he began to take up the vast liquid ocean of green and blue, and then began to grow; as he took in the vast cerulean atmosphere, he grew; as he took in the vast ocean of sunlight, he grew; and left the world decaying, dying, as he now stood, a monolith as big and wide as the highest mountain, and covered in dense multi-layers like the earth itself: a hard crust, the mantel, the inner and outer core, and slowly growing, taking the world unto himself, to remake the world into himself, to shrink the world to himself.

* * * * *

The world became a slaughterhouse.

It was a new era, where the trumpet blast of violent opportunity arose, and those warmongers, those in the service of iniquity, all prospered in the unfettered chaos, in the crimson conflagration of confusion, in the red bonfire of lust and wanton destruction and utter terror.

For here, life was reborn, but without law, without vision, without moral restraint, and the roving hordes preyed upon the meek and devoured them, and soon devoured each other, until there was nothing left but scattered memories of what once had been a world that had had a passing semblance of sense and structure and sanity.

And after all was said and done, and the destruction of Man nearly won, one man stood before the Source, attired in a special anti-gravity suit, and ashamed that he had been full of the disease of pride and egotism. He did not gaze into its consuming fire, nor did he think about his insatiable hunger, for he did not wish to give it more time than it would rip from his soul.

She stood next to him. Her voice was gentle and soothing through her helmet. "Come, my darling, and sit with me, so that we might enjoy this moment." And her soft hand pulled him to the plush of the thick woolen blankets that were outstretched and anchored to the barren ground, because there was no atmosphere, for it had drifted away, as had the oceans.

He embraced her, and he tried not to think of the horror within, and only of the once-cheerful song of the birds, and the once-heavy rush of the cool autumn wind, and the savory pulp of the fresh, full ripe air that had once been; but he could not, for he knew that the Thing would soon drag him in, stuffing his mind with its vile song, its stagnant air, its rancid smell and taste and feel, which would crush his humanness. "But for how long," he cried in his tormented thoughts.

"I cannot think of now," he said, his voice smothered by a venom of regret that he could not control. "I can only think of It." He lay down upon the blanket and closed his eyes. She caressed his shoulders as he spoke in tones low and full of gloom. "I do not know if It exists so that I must stop It, or if It exists because we are corrupt, or if It merely 'is,' another force in Nature that Mankind must learn to subdue." He became melancholy. "Why did I wait for so long to come back? Why did I fear it? Should I have not known that it was It who had come here? Yes, I knew—and I also knew that others who passed by here never saw the Source, save It and me—why? I have let the earth come under Its cruel dominion because I was weak, because I thought we could stop It; no, I knew we could not stop It, for we are brothers, having the same Mother," and he looked toward the opening. "I have allowed the calamity of wars and starvation and disease and utter chaos to pervade the land because I feared what I must endure: the loneliness, the horror of isolation—of simply being—a world unto yourself in this harrowing purgatory; yes, I allowed humanity to slowly die because I was weak, and afraid, not at all willing to disabuse myself of myself, to endure a profound suffering so that others might live—I did not deem them worthy enough for my sacrifice—and now I must be punished for my sin of omission; O, Joelene, this is why human beings are not capable of rule—they are imperfect, flawed, selfish creatures who should never have authority over another living soul."

She wanted to wipe away his tears, but his helmet prevented this. "My darling," she whispered, her voice tender and strong, "when you are there, think of what you must do, and why and who you are, and how the world is, and who needs you; but O, my love, think of me, for I will wait for you forever," and a tear appeared as she whispered, "among the faithless, faithful only she."

He held her then, knowing that she soon would be gone, along with his world.

"And yet," he sat up suddenly, "there must be something still," and a shock of curiosity swept across his face, "something more than this," and as he stood up, he gesticulated toward the Source, "an answer, a reason, a Creator, a beginning, a cause, order, meaning, something eternal," and he crept toward it, but he stopped short of peering into its swirling, sooty vapors. He turned toward her, his visage aglow with the glow of desire. "I must know, Joelene, if what we do has purpose; so, I will think of all these things of which you have spoken, and I will dream a dream about our purpose for being…"

They embraced, and he held her out from him, his right hand seeking to absorb the tears streaming down her smooth, soft cheeks. "I shall remember you, now, as you are," he murmured, and upon kissing the bulbous window of her white helmet, removed his uniform. She felt a calm settle throughout him. He shut her eyes with a wave of his right hand before her face. "Goodbye, my wife, my love, my life, myself," he whispered, passionately, and then removed his helmet.

He leapt in.

* * * * *

The people of the world had endured the terror of Lewis Ferris for two years, and then finally expired, slowly succumbing to the insane will of utter chaos and confusion.

Before the atmosphere and water had all disappeared by the dissociation of molecules, the people of this planet had built great machines to manufacture these essential substances for their survival. Yet, most of the people died. Wars prevailed. Peace was buried in a shallow grave. Brother killed brother; sister betrayed sister; father killed son; mothers betrayed daughters; husbands sold wives; wives killed husbands.

The Emperor Ferris never listened to the people's desperate cries or stirring pleas, for he stood, suspended, his ever-growing mind oblivious to their petty nature and desires, impervious to their puny weapons, apart from humanity, an entity separated by species and knowledge and purpose; and then he began to dissociate the molecules into pure elements of all things, animate and inanimate; thus, all things once visible, all living things, all the earth, slowly dissolved and were swept into his massive hulk; and when the earth had been consumed, his mind reached out into space, and began to sift through the solar system and split the molecules into atoms, and then usher them down into his insatiable body; soon, the moon dissolved, and then slowly, the sun began to lose its form.

And yet Joelene sat, quietly, next to the Source, full of hope and patience, praying, crying, sleeping—waiting, watching, anxious, full of dread—yet, nothing occurred, day after interminable day.

"It is not reality," Joelene said, observing, with great sorrow, the vast ocean of a sullen, dead horizon, as she lay on the beige, woolen blanket, but no longer attired in the special anti-weather gear and her oxygen helmet, beside the Source. Her blanket no longer lay on a tiny piece of barren land—that was the only remnant of the planet apart from Ferris—of rock and dirt, on the bones and husks of memories of things once living, but now, miraculously, it was a small garden of fruits and vegetables and trees, and a fresh, bubbling, cool spring, and a diffusing white light to bathe her cold flesh; and lo, she did not need much nourishment, for her inner physiology had greatly slowed, as if she were merely in suspended animation. "This is not happening," she mused; "he will come back to me and he will make all things good again; I have only to wait and hope and pray, and soon it shall be as it once was..." She closed her tired eyes then, and whispered, "I am there again; he is home and I am there and we are happy and Mrs. Browning is dying and it is the way it should be—people die and there is pain and sadness and suffering, and birth and love and joy; it is the way of the world." She stopped and sighed heavily. "And I am there again, and I am in misery, but he is with me and the world is not perfect, yet it is order and hope and love, a better place than this; O, come back to me, Rymalone, come home and restore that which once was."

She felt a movement, a subtle tremor underneath her, and then she heard a barely perceptible whooshing of air. She looked eagerly to the Source.

And then, without warning, Rymalone flew out and landed gently upon the soft plush of multihued and perfumed flowers. He lay like an infant, oblivious to the external world.

Joelene, her face awash in tears, alighted to his side, caressing his limp body, soothing his blank expression with her soft hands, speaking words of assurance; and cuddling his head in her bosom, and stroking his thick and dry hair, she murmured these words, "You have come back to me, my husband, my love, my life, myself, my sweet and glorious and brave Rymalone," and she kissed him then. She closed her eyes and let her head fall back. "Come home, Rymalone."

There he lay, still unconscious toward the world, embedded in her pious love; and she, holding him tenderly, nourishing his mind, spoke words of remembrance and duty and sacrifice.

He did not breathe, nor evince signs of life, yet his body did not display decay, but perfect and complete preservation, and in his illuminated visage was drawn in a deep melancholy; and then he awoke.

He opened his eyes and saw the lovely face of his wife, yet he could not translate this phenomenon quickly enough, and he started to babble in horror, his arms flailing about as he lay still upon the green mound. It was a kind of incoherent array of utter despair and revelation seeping from his mind and blowing out of his mouth, his senses bound still by human frailness, replaced by a profound, long cry as she stroked his face and rocked him in her lap, and all the while she was whispering words of solace and love.

Slowly, the wounds of shock closed, tightening the delicate fabric that held together his humanity.

So, softly, like the brush of hummingbird's wings against the rarified air, his words fluttered up to her. "Joelene, I am home," and he fell to rest.

After a long and pleasant sleep, Rymalone awoke, this time in a perfectly conscious state, full of energy and anxious about the state of the planet. He said nothing as she told him of the Emperor, but looked up at the cold graveyard of black space. "His existence has brought disharmony and destruction," he said, forlorn; "he wields power without discipline, without knowledge, without foresight; he is incomplete."

"A messenger who does not bring all of the message is a fool and a slayer of life."

He turned to Joelene. "He does not know that I am here, although I have drained him of his power, for he is of this finite world; he is not yet where I am, and he is past where you are; he is best hidden in the deepest recesses of the black soil until his awakening; but this will never come."

He gasped then, a gasp surging throughout his being, flamed by the innate knowledge that a great transmutation was flickering in the glittering shadows of his soul, a merging of forces that began to propagate in his physiology, as well as his mind.

As she looked out upon the small floating isle that was now the earth, she turned to him and said, with tears in her brown eyes, "Perhaps life can begin again," she whispered to him.

"Yes," he whispered, and pulled back from her, for it had already begun.

* * * * *

There was a soft, blurring, rippling sound engulfing him as he fell away from this mortal bond; he felt himself descend into the minuteness of creation, his vision receding away and his mind expanded to see all the precious worlds before him.

There was an immutable boundary, a nebulous sheath that enwrapped his humanness, a seemingly imperishable layer gleaned from weak physical qualities; yet, he penetrated it and passed on; and, at that very moment, he felt himself freed from the armor and comfort and fragility of flesh.

He felt himself drawing upon the sacred inner place of the atom, yet he felt himself still apart from it, away in another place, as one does in his own head, tucked safely away in the bony shell as he peers out from his eyes into the world; he was safe from it, yet he could live the moment inside the atom, and he could not feel his body or the consciousness in his head from where he dwelt; he did not know what it was that approached the tiny world, be it his mind or his physical body, for he felt neither, yet he was conscious of it and of the current state of the world.

He experienced the dark matter field, saw its massive particles as quantum waves, which felt only gravity and the weak force, interacting with the Higgs field, which imparted mass to elementary particles as they were slowed down by moving through it.

He experienced dark energy, the magnificent engine that expanded and accelerated the Universe, a prevailing force, like a tidal wave of pure power, which flowed ceaselessly like a might river in all directions.

He then witnessed the universe of quantum fields: he saw the electromagnetic field as composed of wave photons; the gravitational field composed of graviton waves; the strong nuclear field composed of gluon waves; and the weak nuclear field composed of W and Z waves; and whenever there was a vibration in one of these fields, lo, one of its virtual particles was produced.

And he beheld the elementary particles—quarks, that make up protons and neutrons, and electrons, their obedient travel companion—passing through the Higgs field and gain mass; he witnessed the constant of created atomic mass!

He observed in wonder as showers of oscillating, wispy neutrinos cascading everywhere, and then gazed at the electron as it surged upward into the next energy level, where it produced one kind of quantum wave, the photon—and then sped away and passed through him and into the nucleus, the strong force that held the atom together; and he could feel its magnificent torrent of power radiating all about as it passed beyond his vision into a blur of other photons. His senses crept closer and swallowed the beauty of creation.

He could see the fleeting photon being exchanged between the nucleus and the electron; he could see the electron wave move in deliberate movements, in a rhythmic dance, twittering around the nucleus like a bird about a flower rich with nectar; he could feel the sublime pull of electromagnetism between the electron and the proton; he sought a message, a coherency, a reason for this existence.

He poured himself upon the quantum darling and rode it. "I must know randomness, understand it, breathe it, share its essence," he thought, and so he merged with the substance of this lepton and began to comprehend its message.

"There is order in this chaos," he cried in his thoughts, "there is reason and purpose and hope, but I must know more," and so he released himself into a photon and rode it into the nucleus of the atom, into the heart of the Universe, into the nebula of the quantum world, and into its very private and guarded soul.

* * * * *

He watched with great lucidity of mind as the great balls of luminous energy, the pions—which were produced by a vibration in the pion field—stretched between neutron and proton, riding a blazing, never-ending, relentless path, back and forth, eternal and selfless in duty in helping bind the nucleus. "Deeper," Rymalone thought, and he flew into the pion's field of power and felt a different composition as he sank into one of the neutrons, into the city of the quarks, into the zoo of six characters of gluons, the stuff that holds together the Universe.

"It is a civilization," he thought, in great wonder as he beheld the quarks—produced by a vibration in the quark field—moving freely about within this hadron, while the busy gluons—produced by a vibration in the gluon field—bustled about inside the quarks in their duty to bind and retain their masters.

He still did not feel a physical body, a presence of sensory stimulation; he was force, somehow capable of consciousness, and able to direct his movements along a network of energy that flowed like a river. He felt supreme confidence in his ability to travel its width and breadth and depth with complete impunity, for he felt as if it were on a rail, which he rode as conductor and engineer.

"It's all so glorious," he thought, "such harmony and elegance, such wonder and devotion to the world, these sweet and tiny dancers, these beauteous workers, so right, so clean, so full of purposefulness, yet," he paused, "is there all there is? Is there nothing that is unseen? I must go deeper still, deeper into their ineffable souls, to find their Creator."

* * * * *

He receded into the luminous and vast region of the gluon, feeling a strong attraction upon his being, a force that spoke of eternity and supremacy. He floated in this pasture of translucent loveliness, drawing near to a distant and swirling conflagration that seemed to hover in a soft murmur of gentleness, peacefulness, and contentedness.

There was a pleasurable warmth about him now as he crept upon it, a warmth generated by the twinkling and curling beams of glimmering light streaming from its breast. He was not afraid of this whirling mountain of fire, for he felt an invitation to enter, an invitation from an old friend who had long loved him but had never shared his consciousness.

He swept in, and behold, he experienced what had once been, before the exquisite pages of the Universe were transcribed and unfurled and created all that is known and unknown.

"This is the Universe," he thought, and his consciousness was in a rapture he could not describe, "an element of the cosmos, a part of its consciousness, a fragment of its nature, a particle that is whole, the last unknown ingredient from which nothing further springs." His mind was fed impulses from the forces within the grand sphere, and they shook him to heights of a sublime joy he could not describe. "Here," he cried, "exists all that has been, all the forces of the Universe, all that was once united so long ago and was burst apart; here is its memory, its blood and bone, sinew and tissue; in every atom there sits a tear from the whole fabric that once was omnipotent ruler, and now grieves—but to unite them all is right and true, for it is destiny that it create itself anew, again, a perfect creation, beyond the knowledge of impious Man."

And then he lifted up his consciousness and beheld the swirling energy of existence all around him: and lo, he heard the melodic hum and felt the enervating hum of the virtual fields, and saw how this unique vibration affected the other fields all around them, and thus would allow a vibration to be subtly escorted into the field of another where it would then assume a new particle-nature—just as malleable characters of clay can easily be changed in form with the slightest pressure; and so, he saw the Higgs decay into W and Z bosons— the particles responsible for radioactive decay: whereas the W boson then decayed into an electron and a neutrino, and the Z bosons, which then decayed into electron and positron; and then the Higgs decayed into gluons, and quarks, and photons; and he saw the neutron decay into an antineutrino, a proton and an electron; a pion decay into two photons or two Z bosons; and W and Z bosons into photons, and one type of quark into another and a gluon; and so on, and on and on, one particle decaying into another, each seemingly composed of disparate parts, but truly a magnificent tree with many multi-branches but the same nourishing roots: one into the other, a constant kaleidoscope of one form lending itself into another, ad infinitum, that what happened now was set in the very beginning, and nothing more had been created or destroyed since the first annihilation of antimatter species. Why, he wondered, why is the wonder of creation so diverse and yet so connected; what was there in the beginning that united them all; had they one common identity, one common ancestor, one common denominator, one common thread, which, if pulled, would usher them all back together to celebrate the grand alliance they once were?

He came back to her then, and she watched as his body reassembled itself, slowly, exactly, creating again his bones and flesh and muscle, forming his eyes and ears and nose until his figure was complete; and yet, for a moment, his form was inanimate, like a hideous mockery of life, a vessel without juice, until the lusterless and placid eyes were awash in a tide of throbbing, luminous embryonic fluid, bursting throughout the structure to pump its vital essence into the cells. And behold, Rymalone was once again a physical entity, reborn by his own will.

His face wore the veil of enlightenment from an audience with the forces of the Universe. His voice was gentle and cooing. "Joelene," he murmured, "though I have seen that which is unseen, and heard that which is unheard, felt that which is unfelt, you are still the most beautiful of all creations," and fell into her arms.

She wept, for she knew that he was on a journey that did not allow the company of mortals.

"I must know," he whispered as he held her tight; "I have seen Creation, and now I must create; I must resurrect the real World." He paused, in deep reverie as he surveyed the world about him; he then continued, melancholy, "I gaze upon our World as if it were in pain, aborted while in a divine labor, never able to give us a Paradise full of understanding and harmony." He turned to her again. "My wife, my love, my life, myself—I in you and you in me—it is the Way of the World that all of us should be as One, a World that yearns to be free. Our World yearns to be whole, yet rests, agitated and vexed, held in a sterile bond by a cosmic cement that holds back the natural processes of the World's inner being. The sky that once was," and here he gesticulated about himself, "the deep flush of its grand and radiant blue fire, seeks its inheritance, a righteous marriage with the eternal void of outer space; and the stars, our Mother, motion to our Planet to come home, to sleep, to dream, to mourn no more over petty and vile matters. It is over, it is done…" And he drifted away from her, her hands raised in an inviting gesture. "You will be with me until the end, and then we shall know the Universe."

She felt an electric tingling as a diffuse light engulfed her, a soft, hazy, liquid of snowy crystals dancing around her; and then she saw that he had lost his physical form again, now forging the appearance of a rage of swirling atoms, a dynamism of energy, pulsing and glowing. She looked about herself in awe and fear, for the materials around her, that stuff which was the formula for the world, began to disappear.

And he began to grow.

* * * * *

The small land surrounding him began to dissemble itself and fly to his presence; the trees collapsed and swept to him, and the flowers and rocks and soil and insects and animals gave up their physical shape and were absorbed into him, each and every one drawn by his prodigious force, inhaled and redistributed by their atomic structure into his outer being; and the air, all that was matter broke down and was rearranged atomically and then they were fed into him.

Joelene watched as her world from above and below and toward the horizon was swept into him; and she could not weep, for she felt that he was restoring all that had once been, and that all of this would be one day forgotten, this error in space and time, cleaned and bandaged and healed by their sacred love.

And how could she question him, he who had traversed beyond the boundaries between human knowledge and cosmic intelligence.

The structure of the great monolith, Ferris Lewis, slowly disintegrated, creating a vanishing path that flowed out like a monolithic tidal wave, sucking every bit of debris into Rymalone, until there was only space and void and stillness, ebony-swept-dripping-emptiness, and the stars and planets.

And Rymalone whirled and sang and hummed, as huge as creation he loomed, hungry still for the homecoming of his brothers and sisters; then the planets, caught in his grasp, began to relinquish their sovereignty to him, until they too circled the sun no more.

And then the whole of the choir of the Universe, the remnants of the sun not cannibalized by Lewis, and the other stars and meteors and comets and asteroids lost their special song, for all were soon hurling to him as he reached across the space-time continuum and took their atoms and rearranged them into his fiery bosom. He absorbed quasars, and black holes, and entire galaxies, and constellations, and all radiation, and dark matter and dark energy, every atom, every field, every form of energy and matter receded into him like children running to the solace of their mother after fleeing an approaching storm.

"Has it been millions of years to accomplish such a union," Joelene thought, her mind electrified with wonder, as she still rested protectively inside the wondrous golden globe of lambent energy, "or has it been a moment of two?" She could no longer see the flickering stars. "It is complete."

He appeared to her then out of the great expanse of atomic power, his skin snow- white and his face incandescent and dazzling with illimitable power; and he put out his hand to her in the midst of the vanquished Universe, in the moment before the final consummation. He took her soft and gentle hand and led her into the essence of his being.

He possessed now all the domain of the Universe and its ingredients, and his consciousness feasted on one recurring philosophy, a magnificent desire that crushed all the glories that seemingly omnipotent knowledge had brought, a thought that had languished in a blind and muted prison since time immemorial. "Unification," he cried, "unification, and then I shall know all." It was then that his mass of mind began to implode, refining, extracting all the non-essential material from him, fusing the essentials of matter into a finer shape, forging a final consciousness, the last pearl, a single golden flame of pure and clean and divine matter.

Every particle of his great mass collapsed inward, in a phantasmagoria of power and rage, closer and closer into the ultimate transfiguration.

The moment came, and the once-immeasurable mass now swirled in an immeasurable, infinitesimally small drop of burning matter, a substance in which all the four forces of the Universe were now one simple, sublime energy.

"Unification!" he cried; he was all that had once been created. "What am I! What! Feel!" he cogitated. "Understand!"

He, who now had the knowledge of the known Universe, had a thought, in a place where time and space no longer had meaning.

The fantastic Revelation built itself inside of him, a bold Truth he could not deny. And then he spoke it, full of Peace and Love and Joy, for he knew that the Holy Journey was at an end.

"I am not God."

And then there came a Big Bang.

And behold, he was the Universe, but was not; he beheld all that was within it, but he did not; he felt all that there was to be, yet felt nothing at all; and then the Universe came into being: a pure form of concentrated energy radiating with an intensity level of heat beyond the scope of human understanding; this fantastic energy, this single force, this single entity, that could only be sustained at this extraordinary level, this pure, clean and virgin force that would exist only for a moment, as a rare blue rose that blooms once in a thousand years—perfection, harmony, equilibrium; but it was destined to lose its sublime Beauty, and in this dense vacuum of gravity, as it expanded and cooled and created time and space, a profound sorrow spread across the burgeoning cosmos, as its elegant greatness and joy fell; and from the highest temple of perfection and totality and unity, gravity separated, and the other forces splintered into two distinct forces: the strong nuclear and the electroweak, which, as the heat cooled further, the weak nuclear and electromagnetic forces separated, and thus there were four forces: gravity, the strong force, the weak force, and electromagnetism, the four distinct forces known to exist in Nature.

The particle nursery began its history that would seed the baby Universe, and it was now here, there and everywhere; and it arrived before, during and after; and it moved slowly, quickly, and instantly: the essence of matter, eager to create all that is animate or inanimate: stars, planets, and life.

He watched as the tiny progenitors of matter, these six distinct personalities of quarks, danced and flowed about in this ever-expanding hot plasma soup; he saw the gluons within them moving back and forth and carrying the force that bound the quarks together; and as this hot froth cooled, the progenitors formed protons and neutrons and their anti-social twins, antiprotons and antineutrons; and then, in a cataclysmic extravaganza of antimatter-matter annihilation, saw that only one in a billion of these protons and neutrons would survive, and from this, form all matter.

And then the Higgs field gave mass to these new formations, and the cosmic clock moved closer to fusing order again.

And that elusive, carefree, scampering electron still flew about, now uninhibited, a joyous rascal refusing to yield to influence, not part of any structured, discipline orbit, a free agent still, a rogue, happy to exist apart, needing no one to feel complete and wanted; and then atoms, the stuff that dreams are truly made of, came into being, after surreptitiously capturing the little negatively charged imp in its orbit; and now, the photon was emitted and absorbed between nucleus and electron when it moved up and down the energy ladder.

But the Universe was still opaque, refusing to allow light and radiation to penetrate its haughty, dark veil, and this steel curtain of darkness prevailed o'er the land, and reigned.

And dark matter and dark energy were formed, and commanded most of the Universe.

Now, stars were born: let there be light! And stars shrugged and breathed form into the new creature that bore it, fusing heavier elements in its fiery bosom, and these gas giants roamed free and uncontested, the first children of the Universe; but little stars, and even bigger ones, cannot live forever, and so they died, but in their explosive death, more gas and debris was blown about, and drifted hither and thither, until gravity laid its gentle, cupped hands upon it and formed yet another dazzling, incandescent, sparkling jewel in the crown of heaven.

Spiral and elliptical galaxies began to form from the swirling interstellar gas and dust of their dead brethren, composed of countless stars, and dark matter, many with black holes in their centers, lurking unabashedly as the killer of all things of matter and energy.

And the solar system was born, out of the life and death, rebirth of stars of diverse kinds: of brown and white dwarfs, and red giants, and supergiants, and novas and supernovas, and neutron, pulsar and x-ray stars.

And so it went on, again, but this time in a fashion accelerated beyond comprehension.

The Good Green Planet took shape and set to orbit around its Mother Sun, suckling like a newborn babe at her warm breast, bringing life to her seas and plants and organisms.

Man and his natural history appeared instantaneously, and then the epic moment arrived.

The world was calm, and the world was innocent when Rymalone Weston Augustine stood, in a great quandary, staring at an ordinary swath of rich soil that inhabited the forest floor.

"Quite extraordinary," he whispered, while stroking his pile of black, wavy hair, "it is as if I intimately know this patch of earth." He bent down and put his hands into the cool ground. Sweat flourished about his skin. His countenance was one of concentrated thought imbedded in a great mystery. "I feel as if I have been here before, that something of great importance happened here," he murmured, and paused, for at that moment, he felt as if the answer were soon to be found. He looked about himself and, for the first time in his life, saw the environment not as inanimate objects, but as fellow travelers accompanying him on a grand adventure. His trembling hands touched a maple tree and dug into the thick, brown bark, feeling the sugary sap, the juice that heals its wounds. "Even the plants," he whispered, "are alive. I feel," and here he began to grow excited, "as if I know what it is to be as they are," and he looked about, "as the animals are," and he looked upward, "as the sky is," and he thought of people, "even as they are." He sat down on the patch of verdant plants. "There is order in the Universe. Yes, there are reasons for pain and suffering, good and evil, life and death, joy and sadness. But what is the purpose? I must know. Joelene and I will search, together, and we will find an answer; and this time—this time—I will stay and not be afraid as we sojourn together to discover the world."

He began to run, in a highly aroused state, when he stopped suddenly, for he felt as if something had just shifted and fallen into place, an unseen, unknown substance, an essence that gently flowed away from him, a sense of wonder that slowly ebbed away from him.

The world felt right. He laughed loudly then, and began to run, very fast, smelling and tasting and living the world for the first time.

"Joelene," he cried, "I am coming home."

-Finis-

Traveling at the Speed of Love

I t is said that at the commencement of time and space, there was one universal substance, one universal energy source, one universal power that soon splintered and produced all the known forces which inhabit the world today. It is said that electrons which have a monogamy of entanglement—electrons that share an exclusive bond with each other and are now as one—will always spin in opposite directions to each other; and it is also said that although these particular electrons may be billions of light-years away from each other, when one electron is being measured for spin, it begins to spin in one direction while pointing either up or down, and then the other electron assumes an opposite spin and opposite direction up or down; if this is so, and it is so, then is it not possible that somewhere, sometime, in the long-ago past, there was one universal power called Love, the Perfect Force, and that it too splintered into an infinite amount of pieces, so that now when two passionate people are so united in mind and body and spirit and yet are a great distance apart, they might activate some magical and mysterious energy that instantly connects their two souls together?

The mission to Mars had been written about and talked about and speculated about for so long that nearly everyone had given up on the notion of actually visiting the lonely red planet, except the most ardent and imaginative dreamers; eventually, it did happen, despite the most vehement protestations from the most passionate gainsayers and the vitriolic attacks from the snarling politicians who railed against it by declaring it too expensive to produce and too little reward to reap even as they practiced improbity with an uncanny acumen that resulted in stuffing their personal coffers with too much filthy lucre while concurrently stiffing their constituency with too few results; yet it is the same experience everywhere, and it is this: in order for a dreamer to achieve what everyone deems unachievable, one must listen to oneself and make the improbable probable, and the impossible possible.

The two American astronauts had blasted off from Cape Canaveral and traveled safely during the long expedition and landed with expertise on the dry martian surface. The stated goal of the mission was to search for precious minerals there and possible life or the remains of extinct life, but the unstated goal that was written in the hearts and minds of the men and women involved in the grand sojourn was to obey an internal decree that had driven them all their restless lives, and that was to go forth and explore the regional wilderness that is the Earth and its other self, the moon, and the solar system and everything that is the great icy wilderness beyond it.

The mission was progressing smoothly, and the two men were collecting data and enjoying themselves as they explored the planet in the silver land rover they had personally built and adorned with stickers and other assorted spangled and sacred paraphernalia from their precious boy-hood. After several weeks of broadcasts around the world, the citizens became inured to the marvel of the astronauts bounding about on the first planet to be explored by human beings and the amazing geological discoveries they were making thereon, so most of them went back to their deriva-tive-based, vacuous-filled, banal existence.

The wives of the two astronauts were in the Control Center every day, and had been good friends with each other even before the launch of the Kitty Hawk IV spaceship. The husband of Felicia Robeson was the senior astronaut, and the husband of Melanie Bloom was the junior officer. The press had begged to interview Felicia every day about the idea of a black man being the first human being to step upon martian soil, but she had merely replied that he was the first man to do so, and that was how she saw him—her man; a man—and being a man of flesh and blood and spirit who happened to have skin that was darker than his companion and who hap-pened to have placed his foot first on the cold surface; but the press could not understand it and so continued to harass her, in the same way an unwanted suitor relentlessly pursues a woman who resists his belligerent advances.

It was during the third month of the mission that Felicia and Melanie were down in the Control Center with the men and women assigned to this mission, and Gene Francis, the executive in charge, was explaining once again, to his great delight, the science of radio waves and the speed of light to the women; they listened politely and with interest, as was expected of them, as they really wanted to, for they deep-ly appreciated the passion of such dedicated people, who were the exemplars of consensus-building skills regarding missions and not practitioners of groupthink or confirma-tion bias. Gene had not evolved his leadership through an autocratic posture, nor did he calmly endure a culture of "yes" or a culture of "no" about him—no, indeed, he stimulated and encouraged his crew to speak their mind and search for answers as a team; for, he reasoned, the lives of men were more important than petty squabbling and petty grabs for power by petty personnel.

The women were even attired in their finest clothes, and though they were here in this room nearly every day—dressing in a pink jacket and skirt one day and perhaps a beige polo dress the next—they reasoned this was the finest hour of their husbands' lives and the finest hour of the crew's and the finest hour of their lives, too, and they would not trample this epic moment in history by evincing slovenliness or accepting to be the lowest common denominator in fashion society.

"Well, ladies," Gene said, smoothing back his blond crew cut and then adjusting his black horn-rimmed glasses, "you see—now, stop me if I am boring you," and he looked at them with innocent and eager anticipation, and upon seeing nothing in their beautiful faces but the affirmation of his query and hearing the pleasure in their quiet voices for him to proceed, he continued on, with vigor, "you see," and he pointed to the big screen, whereupon the ladies could observe the men in their spiffy, crumpled and baggy white space suits, which were crowned with the large and round and bulbous black helmets: and there was Ed Bloom driving the land rover with Joe Robeson sitting next to him, and then Joe stepped out.

"Ladies and gentlemen, back in the control booth on Earth," Ed began, solemnly, waving his monstrously gloved hand as he looked at the video camera mounted on the tripod, "I have just made perhaps the greatest discovery in the history of Mars."

Joe smiled as he lifted up the special fold-out shovel, and shook his head.

Ed stood up perfectly straight, threw out his arms in a dramatic gesture, and then announced, "Joe Robeson is a slob—clothes everywhere, the cap left off the toothpaste—Felicia, if you could just drop by, even for twenty minutes…" Joe bent down and picked up a medium-sized rock and casually lobbed it toward the junior officer, who, by then, was already well on his way toward the ship, merrily singing all the way there.

Joe looked at the camera that he had set before him and then said, wryly, his half-smile barely visible through the thick glass of his helmet, "Guess who is making dinner tonight," and then he smiled mischievously, "I call it 'Martian Surprise'…"

Everyone at Mission Control laughed, and loud and hearty, too; laughter from them that sought many ways to relieve the fears that lived in their minds regarding the Kitty Hawk III mission, which had nearly cost two astronauts their lives and coerced them to abort the first space flight to the celestial body the ancients named after the Roman god of war.

"Eleven minutes," Gene said, still smiling, "he said that eleven minutes ago, and now my reply," and he picked up the wireless black microphone and said into it, in earnest, "Careful, gentlemen, the wives are here." And then he turned toward the women again. "And now, eleven minutes more to get to him—so, after Ed's little witticism and my remarks, it is a grand total of twenty-two minutes for words traveling at the speed of light, to complete just one brief conversation."

Gene handed one microphone to Felicia and the other to Melanie, and then walked away as the women moved into the two separate darkened booths to talk in absolute privacy to their husbands, each of them still watching the large screen that was at the front of the Control Center; the women would speak and then wait patiently for the twenty-two-minute time lapse, and speak again, and then wait patiently again, neither of them reading a book or knitting or engaging in other busy activity, but mostly closing their eyes and resting their folded hands upon their lap—Melanie laying her lithe hands on her powder-blue drop-waist dress, and Felicia laying her lithe hands on her ruby-red dress—and dreaming of being with their husbands; but perhaps no one dreamed harder and with more longing than Felicia, as she and Joe had grown up together and never dated anyone else and were in as much love as they had been when they were just children chasing each other with squirt guns and water balloons on long, hot summer days.

After a long while, the women came out of the booths and came to rest at the brown maple handrails in front of the giant screen and watched in complete serenity as Joe engaged in his mundane martian chores.

"Chief," one of the men of the crew then said, "I've got some movement about thirty degrees up."

"Let's have a look-see," Gene said, and as the image was magnified at the particular point where the object had been sighted, the computer analyzed it and swiftly recognized its nature and then plotted its course. Gene leaped to the microphone. "Joe, get out of there—a meteor is coming; Ed, a meteor is going to hit exactly where Joe is working—get there, man!"

Felicia rushed over to Gene and said in a voice that was still hopeful but straining to stave off anxiety, "Tell me what it means, Gene."

His face was grave and his voice was stripped bare of hope. "I won't lie to you, Felicia—that meteor is going to hit in approximately ten minutes." He looked at Felicia and saw a face that was in denial and attempting to thwart the reality of it all, and when he looked at Melanie, he could see that she understood the full impact of it as she gasped and her hands covered her mouth and then tore into her blond scalp as her blanched face bled true horror.

"But what about the sensors on the ship, why didn't they pick up the meteor; how do we know that there isn't some other explanation..."

Gene wasn't evincing a face that was pliable or amenable to her desire to ignore the facts. "Felicia, the image we saw projected a collision in twenty minutes, an image that was sent exactly eleven minutes ago, and my message was sent and will be received in eleven minutes..."

Felicia was shaking her head as her face reflected a portrait of disbelief. Her voice was rising up in volume and tone to resist the fear that was crashing over her like a violent tidal wave. "No, Gene, no; I don't believe it, no," and she turned to look at her husband, who was working assiduously in the great canyon, Valles Marineris, and realization came upon her, and she could feel an electric shudder numb her body. Melanie came to console her.

Gene could do nothing but wait, and would not dare ask the women to leave, for they were women of space warriors and would never turn away from what they had known might happen one day and knew they must face, or live forever with the regret of being weak and living a lie.

"Maybe he will turn and see it," Melanie whispered, holding Felicia and stroking her long, black hair; "maybe he will."

"No, he won't, he won't turn and see it, not Joe," she whispered in an eerie tone that seemed to portend this conflict, "not my Joe, once he gets to work," and her voice became wistful and strong. "O, when he is engaged in a task, he is of a single-minded purpose and sees nothing else and hears nothing else—no, he will not turn around until he is done with his labor."

"How long do you think it will be to finish what he is doing?" Melanie asked Gene in a low whisper, holding the hem of her dress.

He had to say it quickly and without hesitation to assume credibility. "An hour, at least."

Felicia winced in pain and clutched her breast. "Joe, my Joe," she murmured, and thus, it all began; she no longer heard Melanie or Gene or anyone else in the Control Center, as she was no longer there with them except in physical body, for her spirit had already ascended to a different plane and dimension.

Everyone in the Control Center was drawn to look at Felicia as her emerald-colored eyes closed and her slender hands rose up and clutched her moist hair and settled on either side of her head; her mouth was slightly agape and she was breathing quicker and her chest was rising faster; her countenance was painted in agony and despair, as if her internal mind could see something that others in the room could not see; and she was mumbling, murmuring the name of the only man she had ever known or would ever know, the best friend she had ever had and the best friend she ever would have, her wise counselor and confidant, her lover and faithful companion until death, her darling husband: "Joe, Joe, Joe," she uttered, and with every utterance her voice grew in despair and desperation, as if these utterances had originally come from a covenant that was fashioned from the sacred bond these two human beings, who were now joined as one in mind, body and soul, had established long ago in times of crisis; this feverish utterance that poured out pathos and utter sorrow, a stabbing, piercing grief that only the most ardent lovers who have the most fervent union might experience through the most passionate anointing. "Joe," she whispered, as if she wished the very sweet word to seep through the mere walls and streak through the mere atmosphere and streak through the black vacuum of space and settle into the very heart and mind of her most loyal and loving One. "Joe," she nearly cried now, her slender hands reaching out toward the cold and distant orb, "Joe, Joe, Joe," her plaintive wail filled the silent air, "Joe, Joe," she nearly screamed, and then her heavily perspiring body commenced to slowly collapse.

Gene had begun to move toward Felicia but Melanie had abated his progress as she stepped in front of him and shook her head and showed a visage of some strange knowledge particular to the female species, which he needed now to heed and obey.

Felicia's arms were wrapped around herself and latched onto her dress as she slowly fell to the floor and she knelt to her knees and lifted her head up and toward the red planet. "Joe, Joe, Joe," she whispered, with such urgency and desperation that fear struck into the hearts of those who heard it, as if she who uttered it and everyone else who heard it were now in peril; and then she fell silent, and her entire lithe form trembled, and her breathing became arduous and quicker. "Joe," she nearly wept now, "Joe," and as her head fell backward, those who were there gasped and rose up in shock, for lo, she who lay crumpled before them in grief and lamentations had transformed, and those there who practiced the art of exploring the unknown now entered into a realm that seemed inconceivable.

She was facing the giant monitoring screen now and her body was shaking as her hands reached out once again toward the martian world; but the smooth, dark skin of her face had grown pale, and her bare arms had grown a lighter shade, too, and soon the people in the Control Center knew what was happening, and they became afraid; and upon further inspection, they could see that the skin of Felicia was becoming frosted, and even her hair was assuming a thin layer of white crystalline ice. Gene sought to console the woman but Melanie would not allow him to, and then she bent down and settled next to Felicia, looking into her wide-open, darting eyes.

Melanie clutched her chest and lost her breath as she stared into the face of her friend; her voice was lit by wonder and fear. "Her eyes," she whispered, moving closer to Felicia, "her eyes are not her own."

Gene knelt down and saw that indeed her emerald-colored eyes were now an ardent pool of a rich, seething black, and he whispered to Melanie as he shook his head, "What does it all mean?"

The voice of Felicia was illuminated now by a great power that seemed to drive its burning pitch into the minds of those in the room. "Joe," she said, but somehow did not say, for it was as if the specific utterance of the word had come from her lips but had originated from an unknown universe that had an unknown language that was able to slice through the ordinary barriers of space and time; and she repeated it again and again, the name of her companion and soul twin in an intonation that was unrecognizable to everyone there.

"Look," Melanie whispered, and her hand clutched her own throat as she pulled back to allow Gene to see what she had seen, and then he too fell backward, and the two of them beheld the phenomenon from a distance, for they intuitively felt as if this supernatural event was best observed from afar.

And what did they see that sent them reeling backward from a woman they had both known for so long?

In Felicia's eyes, they now saw not the color of emeralds nor the deep saturated color of coals, but the very stark image of her man, Joe, who was on Mars, tens of millions of miles away; and her face was covered now in ice crystals and her arms too and her hair was white with hoarfrost, and her body was shaking in a violent paroxysm.

"The screen," someone shouted in the room, and when everyone looked up, they gasped, for what they beheld would have seemed impossible only a few minutes ago but now seemed imaginable; for there was the giant image of Joe, still working assiduously and the meteor still approaching him quickly from behind, but standing up halfway now and shaking his head and adjusting his helmet, for the inside of it was becoming increasingly warm, and his hot breath could be seen forming on the inside of the glass bubble in front of his face. He seemed to struggle with this for a minute, and then he abruptly stopped and stood fully erect and looked directly at the video camera that he had placed before him and then he whispered, as if indeed he could see something that was there now and feel something that was coming from far away back home. "Felicia," he cried, and then he turned around and looked straight up into the red sky and saw the space assassin nearly upon him, and he immediately began to flee; and he ran the best he could and kept on running until that gray meteor of rock and metal slammed into the very spot he had worked, and he was knocked down to the ground from the impact and lay there unconscious.

And by and by there was Ed coming up fast on the land rover and jumping off and helping Joe up and then joking that he couldn't leave Joe alone for a few minutes without him getting into trouble; and just like that, the crisis was averted.

Now, Melanie held the weak body of Felicia—who was now awake again and whose skin was free of ice and whose eyes had the translucent luster of emeralds once more—and she and Gene helped her up and the rest of the crew came to her aid until she was strong enough in mind and body and spirit to operate on her own; and during this whole time, while everyone was bringing succor to Felicia, somehow, someway, they produced a particular face that they had not drawn too many times before but had mastered long ago and whose power they understood, one that stated inextricably and irrevocably to the others in attendance that the incident that had just occurred must never be mentioned by them or acknowledged by them to any outsider or even to each other; and just like that, the great seal of brotherhood and sisterhood of secrecy was approved by them in the deepest chambers of their deepest affections for Truth and Beauty and Knowledge and locked away forever in the deepest regions of their heart.

Six months later, the two heroic men came home from their epic mission to Mars and were immediately whisked away for a short stay in the special chamber that would analyze and then normalize their physiological functions; and when they were released from this small inconvenience, Ed walked out and embraced his wife and then looked affectionately at Felicia; and then out came Joe, who, as he came toward Felicia, was walking as if he knew what had happened and had expected to happen: because it was the special bond between them, which had been built on trust and love and confirmed by joy and hope and fidelity, that had allowed it to happen; and so when Felicia fell into his arms, they wept, and then he looked affectionately at Melanie, and nodded, as if he knew she had rendered his wife a great kindness, as if he seemed to understand what had occurred in the Control Room without the necessity of words; and as they embraced each other right there in the hallway of the aeronautics building, it seemed as if this was how they had spent their entire lives together—even when they were apart, they were not, and thus could never be separated—and they would not, could not ever be apart again for the rest of their joyous lives.

-Finis-

The Expanding Earth

The Cromwells loaded their automobile and began their summer journey from Cornwall County to the County of Kent, as they had for ten years, a vacation they earned by working very hard at their place of employment, and by keeping up their house, and incessant visits to local friends and relatives, and clubs, and associated obligations families have, so it was a chance to finally pull away from the constant bombardment of things to do and things to see and people to visit in this hyper-convoluted, never-ending, always-moving Modern Era, and cherish sacred time together, if only in a car. The children were grown now but the family still enjoyed seeing their relatives in Kent and the sights along the way and engaging in games families play on such excursions. The route followed by Mr. Cromwell, with Mrs. Cromwell as navigator, was always the same, and the mileage and time it took to reach their destination was nearly always the same. This time, when they pulled into the long and clean, white driveway of their rich relatives, Mr. Cromwell noticed that the odometer read ten miles longer than any previous trip taken, and Mrs. Cromwell noticed that the trip had taken ten minutes longer, too; now, the

Cromwells were very meticulous people, and more so when it came to trips and household budgets, and they took pride in keeping a very accurate journal of their trips not only to Kent but also to closer Surrey and Hampshire. This longer trip certainly was an oddity, Mr. Cromwell stated to his wife as they got out of the car and began to retrieve their suitcases, but soon forgot about the anomaly when the cousins came out to greet them and the one-week visit commenced.

On the trip back, it took twenty minutes longer than ever before and twenty miles longer. Mr. Cromwell was disheveled now, in mind and body, for he was a very organized and thorough man who did not tolerate unaccountable aberrations in his life. The next day, his trip to work took exactly one minute longer than any previous amount and nearly one mile longer, too, and this, Mr. Cromwell knew, was absolutely and positively impossible.

The next day it took him two minutes longer than anything previously recorded in the twenty-year history of such data, and also an astonishingly two miles longer—and this, Mr. Cromwell knew, even though he had adjusted for traffic and perhaps jotting down the wrong mileage the day before yesterday, was absolutely and positively not possible at all, not today or yesterday or even tomorrow, for he knew, as everyone else knew, that there are many constants in the world that never change so people might rely upon them and focus on them and adjust their internal compass to them and therefore anchor their minds to them in times of chaos, like a pound of meat weighs a pound, and a square has four equal sides, and England was the country he lived in, but now he was being told by his impeccable watch and his ever-reliable odometer that his twenty-year constants were now being pushed out and replaced with uncertainties; no, this did not sit well with him at all. So, he bought a new watch and had the odometer of his automobile recalibrated and then he inhaled deeply and exhaled slowly the next morning as he took off from work with the exact odometer reading written down and the exact time written down next to it. He arrived at work three minutes later than ever and nearly three miles further than ever before. He was so flustered he was unable to exit his automobile for a good five minutes, and this from a man who was so punctual that other employees set their watches around his arrival and departure times.

The trip home took four minutes longer than ever before and four miles longer, too. He sat in his driveway and did not get out of his automobile for thirty minutes. Mrs. Cromwell feared for his health as she stared out of the window and ran her slender hands through her long, black hair. Supper was getting cold.

When Mr. Cromwell finally exited his green automobile and lifted up his brown leather suitcase, he altered his route and walked to the neighbor's home and found Mr. Kinkel and inquired as to whether he had found the general vicinities becoming longer both in physical distance and time to arrive to; well, Mr. Kinkel just sort of wrinkled his thick brown brows and tilted his round head and asked Mr. Cromwell if he was serious or jesting, to which Mr. Cromwell then explained his findings of the past days as it related to time and distance in traveling. Mr. Kinkel nodded his head and agreed that the entire matter seemed curious and perhaps the police ought to be contacted, for certainly they would know if such strange things were going on. Mr. Cromwell actually drove down to the police station right there and then and was told by the sergeant at the desk that, yes, places, in general, seemed to be further away and of course longer to get to, but no, he had no other answers.

The next day it took Mr. Cromwell five miles longer and five minutes longer to get to work, and when he arrived, he asked people there about this phenomenon and they too had noticed the incremental advances, but no one seemed to know anything else about it. The trip home took six miles longer and six minutes more, and when he drove into his familiar driveway, he jumped out of his automobile and ran straight into his house and hugged his wife and children and then poured a cool glass of a calming beverage and turned on the television and listened to the reporters speak of the strange happenings concerning the lengthening of distances around the world—but no, no one had any definitive answers, but at least he now felt at ease, and then he turned and said to his wife, misery loves company.

A month hence and the trip from home to the office took Mr. Cromwell forty minutes longer and a remarkable forty miles longer than ever before; it was all very disturbing, but there wasn't much he could do about it because everyone was affected the same way and everyone had to adjust their schedule as he did, by simply getting up earlier every day to ensure they got to work on time. When Mrs. Cromwell left her home for the post office and proceeded to walk on level ground and did not procrastinate along the way nor spend very much time there, it took her approximately two minutes more to get there and approximately two and a half minutes longer to get back home.

The next summer, the Cromwells got in their green automobile and began their trip to their rich relatives in Kent County, and by the time they arrived there, it had taken five hours and nearly three hundred miles longer than anything previously recorded in their little black book of statistics; the trip home took six hours and nearly sixty miles longer than the trip only a week before. This was the way it was now, they knew, and no one could do anything about it, not anyone, not any scientist nor any political official nor any rich man's money, so they just planned ahead to make sure they would get to where they were supposed to be on time. They were a very punctual family.

Five years later, the trip to Kent County took forty hours longer and more than two thousand miles longer than ever recorded, and the family decided, especially after the return trip was recorded in the little black book as having taken forty-three hours and two thousand and two hundred miles longer than ever before, that the trip to Kent should be canceled in the future. Mrs. Cromwell turned to Mr. Cromwell as the family drove into their driveway, and said, why don't the cousins come here for once?, to which he had no reply.

Seven years later, the walk to the post office for Mrs. Cromwell was now time prohibitive, for last year the journey had taken two hours longer than ever; consequently, she quit that method of delivery, and when she took the family car to shop, she went only once a month now, as she would have to leave in the early morning to ensure she would be back before midnight, a trip that now took twelve hours longer than ever before. She had to be sure she achieved everything she needed to do during this sojourn because she could not afford to go back for one single thing, like having her hair done, because it would take half the day. Mr. Cromwell was now living at his job because if he drove home, by the time he got there he only had time to eat and shower and get right back in his car and drive right back—so, he was living at work, like most of his fellow employees; unlike the others who had simply quit and found employment closer to home or merely quit working altogether.

Ten years later, Mr. Cromwell did quit his job and now he was not working and his wife was no longer attending to shopping unless they needed emergency supplies. The children had grown up and married and moved away—in fact, the boy was still moving away, having now been on the road with his blushing bride for two years as they drove to the next county.

The Cromwells were living like most people around the world now. They were living in a self-sustained existence, growing their own food and making their own clothes and keeping many animals on their ever-growing acreage. Most of their neighbors had drifted so far away that it was even difficult for the Cromwells to ride their horses over for a visit, unless they gave themselves the entire morning for the affair. Such events were a great joy and every moment was savored and celebrated, just as if it might be the last such time they would gather and talk of the old days and the old ways and now of the new days and the new ways.

There were now no wars and very little crime and less pollution and disease and really no countries anymore and no states or cities that were functional; at least that was what the television stations reported, at least those stations that managed to send out a signal and could at least cite some credible source for their statistics; but soon, even these lone stations went out and soon there were no functional electrical grids and no gas lines and sewer lines and pipes for water into homes, and so people were either living in solitary existences and manufacturing everything they needed and occasionally taking long trips to abandoned shops for supplies or occasionally raiding a neighbor's home, or living a nomadic existence until they found their far-away destination.

Mr. Cromwell and Mrs. Cromwell were standing in their backyard and observing that they could see no human being or manmade physical structure within their sight. The golden horizon lay before them in the seemingly increasing distance, and they could see mostly barren land and trees and plants, but really could hear no sign of human life at all. They held the hands of each other and then sat down on their white wicker chairs and took up their cold glasses of tea and gently touched the glass of the other, and they smiled with joy, knowing they had each other, and no amount of geographical lengthening could change that.

-Finis-

The Vision

He was never a man who listened to anyone's theories or read any profound literature without doubt first courting him like an obsessed mistress, and then he would scrutinize everything he had absorbed and cross-reference the new information with every bit of pre-existing knowledge in his ever-expanding and magnificent knowledge base; and consequently, he never trusted anyone or anything without this scintillatingly sharp razor of mistrust seizing the essence of the person or idea and then chopping it into finer bits and pieces and squeezing out its vital juices and straining it through his prodigious intellect until all that was left was the empirical and falsifiable evidence; and consequently, he rarely believed in anybody or anything because most things and most people in life need at least to be wrapped in a little bit of faith in order to survive in the mind of a person.

"Religion," he said one day to Thomas, his closest friend in the university, "is a manifestation of a culture's lack of intellectual stamina, an artifact from ancient times that was an unfortunate but perhaps necessary conceit for an ignorant age—a myth, a superstition for savages who feared the

natural processes of the world that became a soothing blanket they could wrap their trembling bodies around and gain
some degree of solace to explain the world, to appease their
desire for origins, and give their desperate lives a little bit of
meaning." He smiled as does one who was born after a tragic era and has read about the mistakes made therein and is
certain he will never make them. "But now we have our own
verifiable religion—science."

"But isn't it possible that even in this modern age, a religion might be born?" Thomas returned. "Look at how many
people are affiliated with organized religion today."

"I am sure it is possible, Tommy, my boy," he said,
euphoria being the surging power that bore up in him,
that undeniable and indefinable feeling that commits one
to shouting to the world that you are alive and know the
answers to every dilemma ever conceived, "but look at the
majority of religions—at least the major ones—that began
when people did not have what we have today to research
and help us think about such impossible things: comput-
ers, instant access to information across the world, scholar-
ly books on every idea imaginable, television and radio; it
would be very difficult for a new faith to begin now without the scrutiny of the media; no, I am just afraid that the
hucksters and hoaxers with their supposed miracles and
claims of divine revelation would be thoroughly investigated and debunked. Well, you know as well as I do about
those preacher–con men and their secret microphones
and confederates and how they got caught?" He smiled in
his arrogance, as if he knew what would happen if anyone dared proclaim a divine revelation today. "I mean, is
religion any different from a political party that someone
belongs to," and then he said the next three words like a
child would, "'because their Daddy' belonged to it and his

father before him and ad infinitum, a typical non-thinking individual who is a ripe candidate to join a religion—and certainly these people have never truly thought what their party really stands for, which is frightening enough."

"And yet, religions do start, like the Morriseys."

"Yes, you're right, but they are more like a cult—a new religion just cannot flourish today; it would end up with a small group of adherents, like a cult." The force of his argument seemed unimpeachable to him because he was acquiring new information and knowledge so quickly that he felt as if he were becoming an intellectual superhuman.

Thomas, his curly brown hair falling over a tanned forehead, which sat high above a set of white and straight teeth that sparkled whenever he issued a pleasant smile at a pretty co-ed, smiled in a way that signaled private knowledge about a topic someone has just mentioned—yet, it was not smugness, for his comely face radiated brotherhood, still.

"All right, Tom, what is your neuroscience team at the university working on that has to do with this? Cone on now, don't hold out on me—not now, boy-o!" Benjamin Israeli said, laughing.

His playful smile widened. "It's about the brain, Benny, ol' boy, manipulating the brain to see how chemicals are involved when people experience religious phenomena."

They discussed this scientific theorem for some time, and then Thomas enquired about the PhD program Benjamin was enrolled in.

"So, how go the Greeks: do Socrates and Plato and Aristotle still amuse you?"

Upon this philosophical issue, the two graduate students conversed for some time, and after interlocking the two stubborn horns of science and philosophy together, each youth—iron sharpening iron—felt exhilarated during the discussion, much like a person feels after they have labored good and hard in the boiling sun and a cool rain falls upon him.

"So, Benny, would you like to come by and visit Dr. Corcoran again? He still talks about your last visit—'very intriguing,' he called it, his highest compliment, you know. We will be conducting experiments contrasting the sensory world with the perceptual world; volunteers get fifty dollars a session—are you game?"

Ben smiled. "Will I become a trained assassin after it's over?"

Thomas laughed. "No, but we will work on your shyness with women."

The smile upon Benjamin dropped, as he mused upon a flaw he could not presently surmount, and then he said, melancholy, "Sure, anything for science."

Dr. Corcoran, head of the neurobiology center at the university for twenty-five years, was directing his postgraduate students in the conducting of experiments that were related to the functioning of the brain; specifically, how the brain perceives images and how those images are stored; how the cells in the brain come together to produce a specific behavior and how the environment affects those cells; how the mind influences human beliefs and practices; and how the biological systems and behavior affect one another. When he beheld Thomas and Benjamin enter the laboratory, his visage expressed a brief joy as he approached them and shook the hands of the youths, and then bid Thomas to resume his work and bid Benjamin to walk with him as they toured the busy place together.

Dr. Corcoran talked of the advent of science shattering the final walls of ignorance that early Man had resurrected to explain the cosmos, that the fate of Man had been determined long ago, and therefore considered himself a proponent of determinism; and Benjamin talked of the advent of philosophy in exposing Man's inherent weaknesses to appeal to the easiest and simplest explanation for any event, and how philosophy sharpens the intellectual tools a human being possesses so not even pseudoscience might fool him, and declared that Man can determine his own course in life despite the past, and therefore he considered himself a proponent of free will.

Benjamin declared that he was more of a humanistic naturalist and a pragmatist, that he embraced empirical methods and hypotheses and research to help decide if something was true or false; and Dr. Corcoran declared that he was more of a reductionist and universal mechanist, believing that all physical processes could be broken down to their basic essence—that which they were made of—like atoms and molecules, and once these building blocks were identified, the human body and mind could be altered through manipulating chemical processes and the like.

"But scientists are the most easily fooled of all," Benjamin said, smiling now, as it was late in the conversation between the two men, and such teasing was permitted and even encouraged to provoke the honesty in each of them. His voice was smooth and his cadence fast as his great mind flooded his mouth with a fast and furious bundle of lucid thoughts and facts. "Scientists are notorious for allowing magicians to dupe them into thinking said magician really does have special powers because the scientist is blindly following a checklist and if the magician successfully navigates it, well, there you have it—now people really can move objects with their mind because there it is in black and white; come on, Dr. Corcoran, how can a real scientist believe in kinetic abilities just because a charlatan moves an object in what looks like a controlled experiment but really isn't? Science fails us when we don't consider the limitations of either people or Nature in these experiments. Am I right?" He really did not have to ask the last question as he thought he was right long before he had walked through the laboratory doors and long before he had met Thomas and long before he had come to this university and majored in Philosophy and Political Science and impressed all of his professors to the point that they wanted him to immediately acquire his PhD and shortly thereafter commence teaching on campus; his mind had always been his greatest asset, just like sharp teeth and powerful jaws are the greatest assets of a mighty lion; and as he grew, his mind grew too, building him an intellectual armor that would easily repel shafts of ignorance but was still not solid enough and strong enough to recognize and defend against sophisticated weaponry, but in its infancy and immaturity it thought it could, and this was the part that put its master in peril.

Dr. Corcoran smiled in the same way a father does when he is pleased that his son has recently discovered a basic truth in the wide, dark world. "Benny," he said, putting his arm around the youth, "you're getting brighter every day—exponentially so—but all work and no play makes Jack a dull boy." Hot and delicious meals were brought in by lab assistants as the white-haired, elderly widower, who had no children, and the handsome youth, with a mind expanding like the baby universe, shared the scientific and philosophical history of humanity. Dr. Corcoran was impressed by Benjamin's bold, new, unfiltered interpretations of all academic fields, and Benjamin, although supremely sure of himself, was too often rebutted in principle and theory by his mentor.

"So, Ben, you really believe an intellectual would not be taken in by the kind of tomfoolery that you allude to by magicians?"

"Absolutely not!" he returned. "Not a true intellectual, anyway; I mean, sure, you might make a few clinical errors at first, but no: no real intellectual would believe in a man— well, for instance—who says he can levitate an object," and here the bold youth stood up abruptly, with arms folded defiantly, "prove it to me right here and now, I would demand," he said, firmly, "right now in my laboratory and under my rigorous conditions, and that fool would just sit there—or stand— and do nothing because there would be nothing to do!" Now, he was laughing. "I've investigated hundreds of such episodes of people who claimed to possess supernatural gifts—healers, mind readers, telekinesis, holy visions, ESP, astral projection: why, sir, it's all absurd—like alien abductions—fakery and fake footage; now, thank goodness, once in a while someone comes along and tells the unvarnished truth—like the man who admitted that he and others had faked the Nessy head and photograph that helped perpetuate the lake myth, or the fake photograph of Bigfoot, or even the crop circle confessions, which, unfortunately, did very little to damage the enthusiasm of the ordinary citizen who still looks for the extraordinary to still believe in, and all because people so desperately want to believe in the lost magic of childhood!" He had stated all of this as if Dr. Corcoran had never heard such a dynamic denunciation of these phenomena before.

"And ancient aliens!"

"That too," Benjamin returned, laughing, smiting his thighs, "how rich was that! The man admits it was all a hoax and yet people still believe it—amazing, Dr. Corcoran, absolutely amazing, what people will believe in; it is as if they have to search for that supernatural element somewhere, find it, and then establish a ritual so they might worship at its sacred altar."

"But not you, Benny boy…"

"No, no, I wouldn't say it isn't impossible for me, I would just need to have it proven to me."

"Of course you would, Benjamin," said the professor with the white beard, and then acknowledged his pupil with a knowing wink.

Spring arrived and with it came the false promise of a Winter vanquished forever and the promise of new tomorrows and endless possibilities as the warm breezes that carried sweet perfumes and fine music melted frozen images and thus allowed the people to come out of their hibernation and let their weary bodies bask in the golden shafts of energy; and for Benjamin, from the beginning of the Winter solstice to its final humiliating abdication and martyrdom to tepid Spring, when not mastering the finer points of oratory in his speech classes, while not reading the great speeches from the last two thousand years, while not thrilling the student body on campus with rousing soliloquies about controversial topics and convincing them that yesterday he was wrong and now he was right; and then thrilling them the next day by taking the opposite view and convincing them again he was right; and then returning to the first position the next day, and smiling in private smugness at how he could easily manipulate people with his rare gifts of persuasion, had visited Thomas and Dr. Corcoran at the laboratory nearly every day, feeding his intellectual appetite and engaging in more of their brain experiments. It was a particularly delicious warm and fragrant night in April when Benjamin, sleeping soundly, was startled to awakening, and then abruptly sat up in bed to behold a glowing image he knew, even in his blurred senses, was an artifice.

"Fantastic," he whispered, staring at the hovering, silent human-looking creature in his small apartment room, "I am dreaming wide awake and yet this seems so lucid—fascinating!"

"No, Benjamin Israeli," lovingly whispered the fair-skinned man, dressed in the luminous, flowing white robe that showed his bare white feet, "you are not in a dream, but in the presence of an Angel of the Lord."

"Oh, ha!" Benjamin articulated, much amused now, and instantly reared up and ran straight into the vision, but merely passed through its radiant figure. "Incredible—a perfectly delightful hologram in my room; kudos to whoever is behind this sophisticated hoax!" He was not the least bit frightened.

"You are an unbeliever," the gesticulating Angel said.

"Thomas! Thomas! Are you behind this? You prankster! Fantastic! What a prank! I am jealous and honored," he cried, and bowed toward the effulgent figure.

"God has chosen you, Benjamin Israeli, to be the messenger of His sacred word to this fallen world."

"O, bravo! The plot thickens! But really, Thomas," and his voice began to fall an octave as he looked around the room, "come out, come out, wherever you are…"

"Yet, you will soon believe."

Benjamin shouted, "Oh, stop the gag now—show yourself, ye villains!"

But nothing came out except an uncomfortable silence that settled upon the skin of the youth like creepy, crawling bugs.

"All right, all right, I give," he shouted, still looking about for confederates, and then to the apparition he said, nodding his head and evincing an apathetic and bored frown, "convince me you are from God—tell me what I am thinking." He cupped his mouth and shouted, "That will put an end to your shenanigans, Tommy boy!"

The Angel let his round, snow-white-haired head cock to one side as he stared at Benjamin with a contemplative stare, and then said in a mournful tone, "No one knows X-2-3-eight ball hot dog banana hey what do you Jupiter grew putty impossible quotient."

A yellow-beaded sweat broke out on the skin of Benjamin as he trembled and his face shook with indignation and rage. "Impossible! Trick! Trick! No one can read minds like that! There is no God! All right," he shouted, panicked now and fumbling to regain equanimity, "take me to the moon right now—right now, you insufferable quack-charlatan-magician!"

And right there and then, right before him and underneath him and all around him was gray barren soil and rock and lunar potholes and an icy, black void, and he experienced every slow and fast molecule of it. After he was back in his room, he screamed like a man shot in battle. "Deceiver!" He pointed at the Angel. "Trickster!" His brown eyes, bubbling with consternation, were widened by hot rage and steaming vengeance. "You have done something to make me hallucinate! Oh, yes," he cried, his face lit by certitude, "predict the future—what will happen tomorrow; you can't do it, you cannot, you faker, you huckster," and his voice settled down into something more calm, "because you are a false equation."

"Tomorrow, at exactly four o'clock in the p.m. in your time zone, an earthquake in San Francisco will occur, and it will rate 6.2 on your Richter Scale; but by the grace of God, no one will be hurt."

"Liar!" he charged. "Come on, Thomas—where are the cameras?"

The Angel vanished.

The next day, at exactly four o'clock in the p.m., a 6.2 earthquake, as measured on the Richter Scale, occurred in San Francisco, and when the television newscaster said that "by the grace of God no one was hurt," Benjamin, watching the show in his apartment, sat stunned into a disturbed silence for the rest of the day, and cogitated upon the events that had recently transpired, extrapolating to the exclusion of food and drink and rest, collecting all available data and seeking to assemble it into one smooth puzzle—but the pieces of the puzzle would not fit, and he was shaken asunder. He had accepted the illusion of the Angel and had been disturbed by the mind-reading and the problem of the moon landing, but when the earthquake hit at the appointed time and place, he grew more pensive, as he could not believe in anything supernatural, even when generous amounts of proof were laid bare to his wide-open senses; yet he was slowly being swept away on the naturally occurring vapors arising from the lingering doubt in his ambling mind—smoky vapors escaping from a now smoldering intellect that had been built upon the trusty resolve that science is able to confirm or deny all phenomena, and philosophy to provide the requite thinking skills and intellectual structure to examine and understand such grand illusions.

He trembled at the mere thought of sleep the next night. He told no one of his Vision. But gravity soon bent even his youthful limbs to the soft sheets of his bed and closed his eyes with airy feathers.

The ethereal voice awakened him. "Behold, Benjamin."

He awoke in a start, and leaped out of bed, staring once more at the angelic creature.

"Go away, you false phantom! You're not real!" His body was already flooded with thick sweat and fear pheromones.

"Benjamin Israeli, God has chosen you to deliver His holy message to this lost world."

"Well, let him tell them—I'm no messenger boy! All right, tell me," he screamed, "what I am thinking about right now, you computer-generated, holographic impostor!" And he shut tight his eyes for a moment and then opened them, but the Angel did not respond. "Ha! You failed—charlatan!"

"You thought of nothing, Benjamin."

Benjamin cursed. His voice was ripped with power and arrogance when he chided the specter, "Take me back about ten million years, I want to see…"

In an instant, he was standing amid fertile green pastures and smelling perfume-scented flowers and watching two brown brontosauruses munching on lush vegetation, and he clearly saw all of it and he bent down and picked up a blade of sweet grass and tasted it and then boldly walked over to the behemoths and in slow, mindful strokes, petted them as he heard their measured breathing and felt their muscular bodies. And then he was once more back in his room. His voice was drained of power, his face blank when he uttered, "I do not believe, no, I cannot believe in any of it, it is a carefully constructed illusion—so, tell me, you ridiculous hallucination, you absurd idea, what will happen tomorrow, and make it good…"

"Tomorrow, beginning at eight o'clock in the a.m., there will be a panic in the stock markets around the world." The angelic visitor vanished.

Benjamin lay upon his bed, drenched in the perspiration of melancholy, uttering over and over again, "Illogical, absolutely illogical, all of it, illogical, illogical, illogical," until he fell to rest.

At exactly eight o'clock in the a.m., the stock markets around the world began to crumble as surely as if they were a chunk of aged yellow cheese, and panic and uncertainty were a pack of ravenous rats. Benjamin had not slept much, but when he had slept, he dreamed of the Vision, for his logical mind, which denied all things supernatural, could not explain this enigma, and tiny fissures began to appear in this carefully woven construct; and so, when the stock markets did collapse as predicted by the celestial creature, his intellectual opposition to the Angel collapsed, as he was beginning to see that there was no way around explaining this supernatural phenomenon into the crowded graveyard of debunked mystics and charlatans.

He attended classes but failed to take adequate notes, he took exams but failed to properly address the questions, and sat in his apartment in the dark, all the while analyzing and reasoning and debating the presence of this arcane appendage to his private sanctuary.

The next seven nights, the Angel appeared and always Benjamin challenged it to do the impossible right there and then, to wit: "Change me into a donkey!" It did. "Take me inside an atom!" It did. "Take me into the future!" It did. "Tell me the future—and not some ridiculous world calamity: make it personal and local!" It did—and with one hundred percent accuracy, too—yet every time it did, Benjamin responded then or the next day, "I do not believe in you, you technologically advanced fraud!" He even attempted, on the sly, to set up a videotape of the events, but he found that the video camera would not work while the Angel was in the apartment. He cursed madly. And still, he told no one of the Vision.

On the tenth night, the Angel once again materialized before Benjamin, who now welcomed it—just as if it were a pizza delivery boy—with a bored look upon his countenance.

"Benjamin Israeli, you have been chosen by God to be His messenger to this lost generation of souls. Do you yet believe in Him?"

There was a bothered look upon his face and irritation in his voice, "Sure, sure, sure—but, no, no, no, no—no way—and what God, by the way? Whose God are we talking about here, huh? And why me, an unbeliever, a skeptic, a sometimes agnostic—worse yet, a lifetime member in the elite club of atheists? What do you want? Why don't you just go on a television show and tell the world about all of it and leave me alone and let me get some sleep," and then he screamed until his voice gave out, "and let me get some precious sleep, you bothersome apparition!"

"The Lord uses the hearts and minds of men to deliver His divine message, and here is the first scripture you will declare before the world: 'I am the God of the Universe, never revealed to Man, the One True God.'"

"A new God?" Benjamin cried, slapping the sides of his aching head. "For goodness' sake, what happened to the old ones? Can't you just make it easier so the people would be able to recognize your boss' résumé?"

"There are no other gods, only the God of the Universe, and you shall record His divine will for Man."

He shook his head and spoke in clearly enunciated, defined terms, "You are not real, your God is not real, this whole illusion is not real; I have been drugged or have gone mad or am the victim of the most elaborate hoax in human history; so, no, I will not record anything. Go away."

"Man has searched for the eternal God since time immemorial, and now the One True God has finally revealed Himself; He must have a prophet."

He frowned. "Prophet, really? But why now, and where has this God of yours been all this time while we have been gorging ourselves on wars and avarice, madness and mayhem?"

The Vision vanished.

For one more month the Angel appeared, and for thirty more nights Benjamin argued against the possibility of it; but his sleeping pattern was no longer arrested, nor his schoolwork retarded, as the Vision was merely another recreational endeavor in the life of the youth.

"I need physical proof, here, that I can see and feel," Benjamin said one night to the Angel, and rather pleasantly, as he now desired these sessions with his hallucinatory visitor.

"There is a woman, Dora Waters: she is stricken with cancer; place your hands upon her and pronounce that the God of the Universe has healed her."

"Dora Waters," he said, anxiously; "I know her; she has been ill for months, but I don't know about meddling…"

The next day, Benjamin approached the college sophomore and without any prelude to his actions, placed his hands upon her pale temple and pronounced the mystical words the Angel had instructed him to speak. She slapped him.

A week later, she came up to him, sobbing, shaking, embracing him and dragging him to the ground as she whispered, "I am cured, I am cured, the cancer is gone, it is gone, I am cured…"

Benjamin sat with her and held her and felt her sincere joy, but his mind was still clouding the idea that this incident was divine.

He went home that night and analyzed this healing with his analytical and logical mind and decided that indeed it was a coincidence or that the girl was a confederate or that it was genuine, but when he cross-referenced this latest miracle with the other miracles, he was coerced into a finding that he abhorred. "Miracles are an abomination, an artifact of ancient man," he said to himself; "they have no place in the world of falsifiable science; there is Nature and Man, and that is all there is—no genies or gnomes or sprites, no aliens or phantoms or superstitions, or dinosaurs living in sequestered parts of Africa; no Bigfoot, no Loch Ness monster, no crop circles, no psychic healing, no palm reading, no astrology—only science—good hard, empirical facts; and this Angel and his bag of sophisticated tricks will be found out soon, or I am mad, perfectly, totally mad or am being drugged, and then I am still right." He smiled, for he knew that he was right and could not possibly be wrong; and then he thought of his mother. She too had cancer and was dying, slowly and surely, and her illness was able to be perceived by his physical senses; and then he felt his supremely strict and disciplined senses peel away and leave him exposed to unprotected emotional stimulation, and he fell completely and utterly apart and wept like a little boy whose mother is dying—from cancer—yet he was still a man who, even though he understood her illness was real, knew that her type of cancer was a death sentence and no kind of science or miracle could help her. She would die soon and he would have no one else in his family. He did not know how it occurred but he found himself praying for the Angel to appear.

The Angel appeared once more as he lay in the solitude of his bedroom.

"O, Angel, my mother has cancer," he pleaded, unshielded by his analytical lens. "God will surely heal her."

"God is pleased with you, Benjamin Israeli, but first you must deliver His divine message to Mankind."

Benjamin sat still, pencil and paper at the ready, and listened intently as the Angel spoke; for seven successive nights the Angel appeared and delivered the divine revelation of the One True God.

"Now, go forth, and spread this gospel of hope and truth to the world, and let unbelievers and those who oppose the One True God be admonished, that the solicitor of death may escort them to the digging sepulcher," the Angel said.

And as he had done every night for seven nights, he asked, "Will my mother be healed?"

"God will bless you and your family." The Angel vanished.

The next morning, Benjamin went to Dr. Corcoran to tell him about the Vision, and Dr. Corcoran, arms folded and his face somber, listened attentively.

"Ben, this sounds like a very complex and very disturbingly well-thought-out illusion designed to challenge your assumptions about the validity of miracles and the supernatural, and in doing so alter that perception."

"No, no sir, no, that cannot be—don't you see, sir, the Angel passed every test: I used forensic reasoning—sir, I really did; I treated this whole affair as if it were a legal case and then applied every known kind of natural law and reasoning and analytical thinking to it and the Vision passed every time—so sir, what else could I have done to challenge the creature?"

"Is it not possible, son, that the final act was to draft the fact of your mother's cancer into this tidy drama?"

After Benjamin declared an emphatic "no" to this query, Dr. Corcoran put his arms around the boy's shoulders and began to escort him toward the laboratories and said, assuredly, "There are more things in heaven and earth…" But then he abruptly and without warning fell violently to the floor, and Benjamin attempted to help him, but it was quickly apparent that Dr. Corcoran was, despite the pleas of Benjamin to the Angel and the efforts of the paramedics, dead.

"You did not believe," Benjamin whispered to himself as he watched the body of his mentor being wheeled away toward the ambulance, "but I will not fail to convince others, who were much like myself—intelligence that masked arrogance and lacked wisdom, an invention of the modern information age, a shallow groove in the well of knowledge; but O, that will soon change."

In his next class on campus, Benjamin stood up and declared the divine message of the One True God. The professor promptly ordered him out of the classroom. Students who knew Benjamin and understood his hostile skepticism toward all things supernatural exited the class early to accost him and prod him for an explanation: and soon there was a huge crowd outside of the building, and Benjamin found himself upon a wall of red brick, relating the story of the Vision. The campus newspaper interviewed him. He told them everything.

That night, Thomas came to the apartment of his friend but found no one at home, for Benjamin had already begun preaching the divine text of the One True God in the city, where his sermons were attracting great throngs of people; and then, that merciless bloodhound— intrusive, arrogant, wall-of-flooding-filth that builds every time they open their vacuous, black mouths—the media arrived, and soaked up the carnival-party-like atmosphere and seized the story with its sharp, bloodied talons and began to shape it into its own enlarged, malignant image. The police came. Thomas came, too.

"Benjamin, we have to talk," he said, pulling his friend away from the smothering reporters.

"Do you believe in this sacred Vision, Thomas, my good friend?" Benjamin asked.

"No, Ben, I don't, because I created the Vision, with Dr. Corcoran and his associates—it's all been contrived, Ben; come, let me show you."

Ben's face was melancholy, his voice serene. "I understand why you don't believe, you were like me—but the Angel passed all the tests, Thomas, every one!"

Thomas shook his head and his voice grew desperate. "Don't be someone else now, Ben, not now—you were in a lab, a lab: you agreed to all of this testing; we have been altering your perception of the world, but Dr. Corcoran died—a death that does not make any sense to me, even though he did have high blood pressure and this whole experiment was very stressful for him, but still—before he could tell you—we were monitoring you the entire time so you wouldn't," and he gesticulated about the swarming hordes of people who were still buzzing around the perimeter of the small area the two men inhabited, "manifest this spectacle!"

Ben shook his head. "I don't believe you, Thomas, I don't—I cannot, for I saw too much; I believe, and for once in my life, it is good to have faith in something other than the finite and corrupt mind of man."

"No, Ben, you must come with me before it is too late," he cried, and he turned toward the growing crowds, who encroached upon the two men and seized Benjamin and placed him once more upon his rock pedestal, where he proclaimed this holy message:

"To reap the blessings of the One True God: live a good life; love your neighbor as yourself; do not harm others; be generous, kind, loving; help the poor, the elderly, the ill, those oppressed; all people are equal, no one above or below any other; you need not pray to anyone, or anything, only to the One True God; you need not seek a person, a thing to touch, or an idol to worship, but believe in Me by faith, attend my Church, and I will make a covenant with My chosen people; do all that I command of you, and you will be in Paradise, on earth and in Heaven.

"All other faiths were created by Man to serve the needs of Man; the One True God wants Man to be loving and good; the wicked will be punished on earth and in the afterlife, and once they repent sincerely, they too will find Paradise; all men and women, regardless of their spiritual beliefs, are welcome in Paradise, for all people who earnestly seek God, even though they belong to many faiths, are truly seeking the One True God, and none will be rejected, as long as they believe in Me and follow My sacred commandments; for all were created so that the One True God might fellowship with them forever."

Charles Hayward, a reporter for the *Inquiring Skeptic* magazine, who was the most radical opponent of miraculous claims by religious preachers on their staff, and who had debated and exposed countless "tricksters" across the country, had been closely following this story and had proclaimed it as simply another elaborate hoax in a long line of hoaxes designed to fool the gullible public, writing as of late, "just more snake oil, hokum-nonsense, spoon-fed pabulum to a growing percentage of people who want to believe so much in the supernatural that they will dismiss a preponderance of evidence to the contrary," now spoke out, challenging Benjamin to demonstrate a miracle in front of the crowd.

Benjamin merely smiled, and said, gently, "Sir, I know of your unbelief, and your hostility toward my Faith; but I will tell you now," and he swept up his arms toward the sky, "the miracle you seek will be in believing in He who sent me."

Charles replied in a scoffing voice, "That'll be the day, you charlatan-quack; and I promise these people around me a miracle—that I will soon expose you and your sorry movement as more of your flunky opportunists set out to fleece hardworking and decent people."

But the mother of Benjamin Israeli was cured of her supposedly incurable cancer, and when this fact was related in the newspapers, coupled with the promises Benjamin had already told reporters that the Angel had said about her, his followers grew from four hundred to four thousand in a week.

The One True God movement swept across the country like a new crop of irresistible fruit that everyone wanted to taste, and within a month's time it had leaked through the very porous borders and across the shimmering seas, and like tiny filaments had stretched its star-spangled message of come one, come all to the impoverished masses and begun hauling them into its burgeoning family.

* * * * *

Three months hence, and Benjamin, sitting in a hotel room in a distant city, rehearsing his speech for a rally the next day, looked up to behold two masked men lunging toward him. He awoke later in the laboratory of his university, gagged and strapped to a steel chair and surrounded by the associates of Dr. Corcoran. Thomas stood directly in front of him, looking far too old for his brimming youth.

"It all started as an experiment in altering brain activity—truly, that was all it was, Ben—and now you're a prophet," Thomas began, and pointing about the place, "for this new technology, and so, it all ends here."

Benjamin attempted to speak but capitulated to the green duct tape strongly secured across his mouth.

"Soon, Ben, you will understand, and perhaps forgive me." Thomas pulled up a steel chair and sat directly in front of his old friend. "You signed the papers," he began again, and held up the documents, "that allowed us to investigate your brain and its relationship with belief systems and how the mind interprets outside stimuli and perceives and regulates data and stores them." The face of his friend yielded only a feigned disinterest; so, he nodded his head and in his mind turned a corner and then came round again to the start of the narrative. "In the beginning, Ben, in the very beginning we were stimulating visual associate cortices to induce hallucinations in animal subjects, and then you challenged us to do the same in you, and even though I was against it, it was done anyway; and yes, we were able to give you hypnopompic hallucinations—this means you hallucinated while you were awake, but the crucial difference being that we directed what you saw; it was like making a movie and you were the actor but you were the only one who thought what was happening around you was real." He paused and his countenance was covered in the shadow of desperation, and then he held up his index finger and made a circle. "Your eyes are constantly in motion, Ben, your eyes are always glancing about and having tiny tremors, but if you could stop the eye from moving completely, then you would have a phenomenon called bleaching, which means that the images before you would simply disappear; so, based on that, we placed a contact lens with a miniature platform on it and a slide projector on that—I know you can see what is coming, Ben—yes, the contact stopped your eye from moving but we did have certain images on it, too, like the Angel, which would soon fade away; and after we collected data on that, we then implanted a molecular video camera on your retina that was receiving signals from our computer; remember when you wanted to see prehistoric images? We first heard your thoughts aloud, and that gave us time to find the correct images and then program the computer and send the signal to the camera—and it didn't matter how long that image lasted, because we needed only a few minutes at the most." He started to talk quicker, as if he would lose his nerve if he paused long enough to contemplate what he had done. He shook his head. "But something went wrong; somewhere along the line you forget about it all—and only recently, too; at first we thought it was perhaps a repressed memory of these events, but now I believe it is lacunar amnesia," and he held up his hands and created a small space between them, "where you have a gap in your memory about one particular event—this one." He was attempting to produce the proper visage and the proper voice that would penetrate the defiant look of his audience, so now his tone was calmer and his face was kinder. "You see, Ben, Dr. Corcoran had wanted to see if a person could be fooled into thinking aloud without knowing it—it's called 'mind masking,' and it worked beautifully on several volunteers; we would ask them to think about something and then we would tell them exactly what they had thought—because they were thinking aloud the entire time and were unable to know it. I hope you can see this would be a major breakthrough in interrogation techniques." He frowned and sighed heavily. "I know you can see where I am going with this narrative." He beheld the pained countenance of his guest. "The government gave us much of our funding for this project, but then the team agreed that with a strong personality like yours, it would be essential to see if, taking the mind-reading deception one step further, we could gain more advantage over the subject; Dr. Corcoran disagreed and wanted the experiment abated, but the university put pressure on him and so he continued the experiment." Thomas grimaced. "I know you, and I know you find this all hard to believe, but we have ample proof—you just have to be patient." He motioned to one of the lab assistants and she activated the video screen, and then he whispered to Ben, "There were other volunteers, as you will soon see, but they did not last nearly as long as you."

It was all there, in brilliant black and white, the entire experiment explained and documented—how a special room had been constructed like Benjamin's apartment, how a special room with holographs and special floors and ceilings that could project three-dimensional images was built; how special-effects wizards were hired to create every image required; how Benjamin went each night to the lab and was allowed to awaken and then experience his Vision; how the Angel was created and other places were expertly and precisely manufactured; and how certain hallucinogenic drugs were given to him so he might actually believe he was touching and feeling objects that were not there; it was all there, every bit of it; and after some time, Thomas tore away the tape.

"You're insane," Benjamin shouted, "you've created all of this to discredit my Holy Vision!"

Thomas, unperturbed, said, "Ben, think of something right now—go ahead, think of anything and I will tell you exactly what you are thinking." He watched as Benjamin fumed and sat silent. Thomas smiled. "But you can't know—you, you, you—XXL9 ratio L Roman hear it jazz."

Benjamin cursed.

"Run the tape," Thomas said, and an image of Benjamin in his chair, thinking aloud what Thomas had just reported, filled the white screen.

"I don't believe it—but even if you could trick a man into thinking he is thinking silently, so what! And what about the predictions?"

"Benjamin, I am disappointed in you—think, man, think! We had a video camera on your retina that gave you the image we wanted to see—the newspaper headlines, the time of day, the day of the week—and we had the holographic room to create images—your apartment, the college campus—and we had the drugs to induce time lapses in you; Benjamin, we could have sent you back in time a hundred years or forward a thousand years with our technology, and you would not have doubted it for one second because your senses were telling you that all of it was real!"

Benjamin's hardened countenance did not seem to soften, and then he shouted, "And what about the girl with the cancer?"

Thomas winced, his face condemning. "I am disappointed in you, Ben; this experiment should not have changed your intellect—of course she was a confederate," and he turned and yelled toward the door, "Cora!"

Cora came in and confessed to her connection to the fraud, and then exited.

"My mother!" he yelled, increasingly frustrated.

"That, we cannot explain…"

"Aha!" Benjamin's face envisaged victory.

Now, Thomas cursed. "Obviously, this is going to take some time; if only Dr. Corcoran had not died—he was going to reveal all of it to you that day." He leaned closer and whispered, "There are other elements involved, here, Ben, sinister elements that want this data to use for purposes other than research, so we will have to be very careful…"

The videos of the early experiments and the middle experiments and later experiments were played over and over again, and once more for good measure, and then again and again that night and far into the early morning, until it was plainly evident to the clinicians that Benjamin now clearly understood, and they released him from his bondage.

"We have a press conference planned for five o'clock so you can explain how all of this happened; we even have top clearance from the U.S. government, too."

The conference arrived and Benjamin stood before the cameras and reports, flanked by Thomas and the scientists involved in the experiment.

"I am here to tell the world," Benjamin began, looking out among the hushed throng, "that the U.S. government kidnapped me and attempted to brainwash me into believing my Holy Vision was a lie, but I am here to tell you now, it is the Divine Truth, and the government is afraid of us!"

After Benjamin was forcibly removed by two university security guards, Thomas took the podium. "Ladies and gentlemen, we have definitive proof that the entire episode of the Angel was conducted by the university, and with complete agreement by Mr. Israeli." He looked to Benjamin, who smiled slyly and shook his head.

A messenger from the university ran frantically up to the podium and whispered into the ear of Thomas, at which point, Thomas bolted from the conference with his team and ran pell-mell back to the laboratory, where they found that all of the evidence to show the Vision as fraudulent, and even all the paperwork Benjamin and the others had signed, had been destroyed.

"What have we done?" Thomas murmured, looking at the smoking ashes, and then he looked toward where the conference had been held. "Benjamin, what have you become?"

* * * * *

Charles Hayward continued to investigate the One True God movement, vehemently opposing Benjamin at their rallies, in magazine articles, during press conferences, in television and radio interviews; and then one night, he received an anonymous note which stated that if he wished to learn the truth about this phenomenon, he should come alone to room 24 of the Wayfarer's Hotel at exactly ten o'clock in the p.m.; and Charles, being a lone wolf who habitually refused the company of "dolts and popinjays" on stories that interrupted his intellectual reverie and attempted to bias him in some subtle fashion, willingly obeyed.

He knocked on the door of this dreary haunt, which sat on the periphery of town, where all things unfashionable and indefinable are tumbled and dragged by the interminable, centrifugal forces of society; a corpulent but cheery-looking man opened the door, and said, "Thank you for coming, Mr. Hayward," and extending his hand, received the customary handshake generally agreed upon by men when first they meet, and invited in his guest.

Charles said, bemused, "Fancy that—Dr. Corcoran, I presume."

Dr. Corcoran smiled. "You have done your research, ace reporter."

Charles winced. "No one says 'ace reporter' these days," and then, cocking his head to one side, he continued on, with a most amiable air, "and, sir, may I say how absolutely marvelous you look for a months-old corpse."

Dr. Corcoran smiled and nodded. "All part of the mystery," he whispered, raising his bushy white eyebrows, "that will soon be revealed—and to a man with an insatiable appetite like yours, you will not be able to resist hearing the whole, unadulterated story; oh, please, please," he gestured toward the sagging, beaten-apart brown sofa, "sit down in my little home away from the warm grave."

Charles did not stir, as he was not a man who complied with any demand or even suggestion with willing facileness. "Dr. Corcoran—do you mind if I call you Martin? Good, well, sir—Martin—I feel I must warn you—a privilege I normally reserve only for my ex-wives—due to your once-lauded status in the community of scientists: this hoax, sir, this abominable hoax that will presently be exploded into myth and urban legend—a dagger through the heart of Dracula, the curtain pulled back to show the charlatan, one more conspiracy uncovered—has just added another dimension that even I, with all my years of investigative journalism, had not anticipated; well, just look at it this way: the man who chiefly designed the alleged experiment involving this fanatic or

lunatic—or just plain faker—Benjamin Israeli, at once supposed dead, is now alive; and, no doubt," and then raised his
voice to accent his single-minded work ethic, "when I start
to dig, and when I do—and by the way, I never stop until
I find the truth—there will be false death certificates, and
confederates, and crimes most foul." He frowned, and his
voice calmed. "I am disappointed that you would be taken in,
but business is business, and this story will sell millions, and
make me a tidy sum, and perhaps make my magazine mainstream, at least for a little while." He bowed. "And for this,
kind and gentle sir, I do thank you most sincerely."

Dr. Corcoran smiled. "Of course you do not believe, my
boy; and neither did I, until I met the One True God, and
He gave me a message."

Charles smiled, and said, amused, "Hmm—let me guess,"
and with animated gestures continued in a mock, grave voice,
"give all of your hard-earned cash to that false prophet, Israeli,
so you can buy your gold-leafed stairway to heaven."

"Oh no," the doctor replied, in earnest, "no, indeed; but
that I should tell the truth, the absolute truth, which is: that
the Vision was not part of the experiment."

Charles frowned once more, shaking his head. "Martin,
come now; the jig is up—no one would believe such hooey;
it was all explained in the newspaper by the university, along
with a fascinating confession by that young co-ed confederate—even though, I must admit, there are still difficul-
ties I have not worked out, and looks bad for folks like me
who know it is all bunk—so, you know what I am going to
do just for you, Professor? I will humor you for a moment
and give you false hope that somehow you will be believed.
Well, let's see: in the first place, the university said the
proof was destroyed—strike one; in the second place, there
is the curious fact that the other subjects told contradicting

stories—strike two; and finally, none of them mentioned the Angel—strike three. And so, what happened? All of this gave more fodder to conspiracy theorists—or don't you get the newspaper in heaven?" He chuckled in the same way the conqueror does when accepting the broken sword of the defeated enemy.

"I am very disappointed in you, Mr. Hayward, very disappointed, indeed, to make light of my claims, to question my veracity, to put in doubt all my dedicated years of service in the field of science to find answers to Nature's most perplexing mysteries—very disturbing, if you ask me—and oh, by the way," and he leaned closer to his adversary, "no one says 'jig is up' or 'hooey' anymore," and he leaned back, nodding his white-haired head; "you must change with the times, I always say."

He frowned again. "Well, first of all, Martin, and, by the way, feel free to call me Charles—if it's good enough for my mother, it's good enough for a man of your esteemed position—and second of all, what about the thorough description of what the university claimed they showed to that quack, Israeli: videos of him being visited by this prefabricated, phony-baloney hologram, the Angel?"

"Easily explained, my boy—Charles—it's all about money, don't you see? The university gets the majority of its funding in my department from the government, because the research is related to national security; and when the Angel appeared," and here his voice became solemn, and dipped in the narcotic of the fantastic as he leaned forward, "perhaps because our experiment opened a portal to the mind of the One True God," and then resumed his normal tone after he leaned back and stood upright again, "the entire experiment had to be shut down, or we would risk losing our funding; oh," he said, gesturing about, "I saw the writing on the wall,

I did; to be honest with you, sir, I am glad I died when I did—oh, dear, the last thing I needed was a long, drawn-out inquiry: let the younger folks engage in that unpleasantness." He smiled and nodded approvingly to something only he could see. "Oh, the wonderful job they did with special effects to try and fool Benjamin—but they did not: he is too smart for them!"

"None of this adds up, Marty, sorry; we have three parties involved here, and either one is lying, or two are—or hey, a better story, yet: all three are off their rocker; you see, I don't care what the truth is, and to be honest with you, the more perplexing it is, the more shady characters involved, the longer it takes to unwind—but not too long, mind you, the public is too fickle and loses interest too quickly, so you just toss them a few bones to kindle the fire—the bigger the reward; that being said, as long as I find out what it is and print it and sell lots of magazines and make lots of money, and retire to that little mountain cabin and live happily ever after with my new, hopefully not soon-to-be-ex-wife."

"You are an unhappy man, Charles," and here the voice of Dr. Corcoran became severe, "I know that, and I want to help you; that is why I asked you here tonight: you walk in an unbeliever, a scoffer, a debunker of miraculous claims—as I was, sir, I assure you, check my record to separate fact from fiction; but, sir, mark my words carefully," and here, his voice became immersed in wonder, "you will leave a believer."

"All right, Doc, I'm game—show me, go ahead and try and convince me—but I warn you, all of this tomfoolery will just make my article that much more appealing, and make me even more famous, as if debunking and dethroning all those false messiahs in the past was not enough to endear me to the public—the least they could have done was thanked me for exposing frauds in their midst." He shook his round head, frowning. "But, in the end, we both know, as soon as they leave one charismatic leader, like your boy, Israeli—I have to admit, the kid has charm and intellect; he could sell a steak to a vegetarian and make him think it was tofu—they join another; why, taking down these nut jobs is like playing whack-a-mole," he hunched his slender shoulders and smiled, and then continued on. "Say, I wonder if they give the Pulitzer to reporters from fringe magazines," and he rubbed his black-whiskered chin, "so maybe, with this newest twist, I may go mainstream," and his visage was lit up by wonder. "Dr. Corcoran—Martin—you, sir, may have given me the big break I have always wanted," and he bowed again toward him, "and for this, I am eternally grateful," and then smiled like the wily cat who has just trapped the menacing dog, "and the more I think about it, you are a One True Godsend," and then laughed heartily.

Dr. Corcoran, still relaxed and amused, smiled and put his arms around him, and said, with a knowing wink, "Thank me after I show you the proof that will change your life forever," and escorted him to the door of the next room, which he presently knocked upon.

Charles Hayward, not one to be taken aback, due to his singular ability to anticipate the unexpected, was now taken aback, for who should open the door but Benjamin Israeli.

* * * * *

According to historians, it was three months hence that Charles Hayward appeared at a news conference to announce that he was now a disciple of the One True God because he had seen the Angel and experienced verifiable miracles, and had then recorded as a manuscript, from revelations received by Benjamin, a book that contained all the laws and commandments, statutes and ordinances, rituals and prayers, and will of the One True God, called the Enlightened Word. And when he then introduced Dr. Corcoran as a man raised from the dead by the God of the Universe, the press went, quite simply, berserk; and as for the media circus that had surrounded all of this like pacing and occasionally attacking jackals and hyenas near a stinking corpse, the tent got just that much bigger, the rides that much faster, and the clowns and jugglers and trapeze artists that much more daring and exciting.

Within one month, there were nearly one million adherents attending electrifying sermons by Benjamin on hilltops, in valleys, and at beaches; in hotels, and at resorts, and inside stadiums; he visited the poor, the elderly, and the sickly; he counseled troubled youths, troubled adults, and troubled social movements and institutions; he helped the homeless, healed broken families, and set up facilities to bring succor to anyone in need; but for all of them, he not only gave them what can be seen—hot food, warm clothing, and adequate shelter—but things that cannot be seen—spiritual nourishment to sustain them when he was gone, spiritual attire to wear proudly for all to see, and a spiritual house to feel safe in, where they might invite others to proudly dwell. And he was seen on television, in theaters, and on websites; and there were the magazines of the One True God movement, and the books, and the pamphlets distributed by zealous missionaries; then came the movies, the songs, and the radio programs; and there were celebrity endorsements, and Churches built, and more donations rolling in freely and in amounts hitherto unknown by citizens hungry for spiritual guidance and an endorsement of their personal philosophy of unrestrained indulgence; and finally came the budding of power by this new spiritual conglomerate—by investing in other businesses around the world—spreading out like a mushroom cloud after a nuclear blast, for this was what it was: an explosion in the middle of a society caught up in its own dynasty of self-absorption, which was unparalleled in human history, and one which clearly needed absolution from its nauseating and quickly multiplying, out-of-control sins, a fast remedy like a shot of penicillin to clear up a guilty conscience that had festered and gnawed on them, which they blamed on other faiths they condemned as unwilling to adapt to the unbounding freedoms and non-judgmental mores of Modernity; and lo, within six months, there were ten more apostles selected by the Holy Three—the Divine Inner Council of Benjamin Israeli, Martin Corcoran, and Charles Hayward—specifically: a retired Brigadier General from Texas, husband, and father of five, of English descent; a housewife, mother of four, from Connecticut, with a PhD in Political Science, of Mexican descent; a cardiologist from Pennsylvania, husband, and father of five, of Kenyan descent; a current member of Congress from Georgia, wife, and mother of three, of Argentinian descent; a pro football quarterback whose team had just won the Superbowl, husband, and father of four, from Arkansas, of Italian descent; a high school English teacher from Oregon, wife, and mother of two, of Russian descent; a construction worker from Arizona, husband, father of three, of Chinese descent; a young and famous actress from New York, single, of Jewish descent; a thirty-eight-year-old firefighter from Arizona, husband, and father of three, of Native American Indian descent; a brilliant lawyer, wife, and mother of two, from Massachusetts, of German descent; a successful and innovative architect from California, husband, and father of two, of Iranian descent; a billionaire philanthropist, wife, and mother of six, of Indian descent; and all of them testified that they had seen and heard the blessed Angel, and witnessed the accompanying miracles therefrom.

Benjamin became the leader of a religious movement that, by the year 2100, had adherents on every continent and in every country, and a holy book translated into nearly every major language, with Churches recognized by government officials nearly worldwide to worship in, and the zealous ambassadors to spread its gospel, and universities to teach its message that now had five hundred million believers; but it was a message that became increasingly hostile to other faiths it considered intrusive and incompatible to its core tenets, which had been enlarged in the second holy book, *Divine Revelations*, a collection of sayings of the prophet and further revelations from the God of the Universe. Wars of faith in the twenty-second century caused the world to become a raging conflagration.

-Finis-